MW01137879

Paperback ISBN: 1521392145

Wolf's Man

Lynn Nodima

Dedication

To the only person in the entire world that daily supports me in my writing efforts, reads everything, tells me what works and what doesn't, and gently pushes me to get books finished. Love you with all my heart, my Sue Bear!

Please Leave a Review

Please leave a review letting others know what you thought of this book. Reviews help other readers find books they will enjoy. They are so much appreciated by readers and authors!

Thank you!

Want to Learn More About Lynn Nodima?
Visit her blog at:
www.lynnnodima.com

Chapter 1

Janelle stepped back into the deep shadows of an alley, sniffing the air. Bustling pedestrians rushed past her on the city sidewalk, not noticing her still form. So many people. So many cars. So many scents to sift through. For a moment, she thought perhaps she imagined the strong werepanther smell, then a light breeze caressed her face, and she caught it, again. Sniffing several times, she finally located the source. Two men, one blonde and the other brunette, stood on the sidewalk across the street, the blonde talking on a cell. The brunette sniffed to catch her scent. Both were dressed in dark jackets and black jeans. The one on the phone turned to look back up the street. His jacket fell open, and Janelle saw the gun holstered beneath his arm.

The traffic signal at the corner north of her changed to amber, then red. Cars on her side of the street slowed and stopped, while vehicles in the opposite lanes slowly picked up speed. All this was peripheral awareness, while she searched for a way to get away from the two men. She glanced behind her and muttered a curse when she saw the alley ended in a brick wall. Anger simmered, bringing a turquoise glow to her eyes. *It's not enough they slaughtered my pack, now they're hunting me.*

Feeling the charge of electricity dance across her skin that preceded the change, she realized her eyes were glowing turquoise. She looked down at the pavement and struggled to control herself before she shifted and gave herself away. One cat she might be able to fight off. Not two. And not in front of humans. With no other options, she glanced at the vehicles stopped between her and the panther shifters.

A mom with two kids in the back. A harried cab driver arguing with his passenger. Two young women dancing in their seats to the beat of the dashboard radio. A black SUV, windows down, a man tapping his thumb impatiently on the steering wheel, while waiting for the light to change. He smelled different, almost familiar. *That one.* Just as the light changed, she slipped out of the alley. As he started to slowly accelerate, she rushed to the SUV, reached through the window, snapped the button to unlock the door, jerked the door open, slid in beside him, and slammed the door.

Startled, he slammed his foot on the brake. "What?"

"Hey, you!" The shout came from behind and across the street.

Janelle threw a glance over her shoulder and saw the two werepanthers start across the empty lanes on the other side of the street toward the car. "Please, mister," she said, hating the fear that shook her voice, "there are two men trying to catch me. If they do, I'm dead."

In the corner of her eye, she saw his eyebrows climb, as he turned to follow her gaze. When he saw the two men rushing toward them, he whipped around and accelerated, catching up with the traffic, then passing other vehicles. He drove for several minutes. When she could no longer see her pursuers in the back window, she let out a shaky sigh and turned to face the front of the vehicle.

2

"Who are you?" he asked.

Janelle studied his profile. *Adonis in a t-shirt*, she thought, then mentally scolded herself. He looked kind, but with humans, you never knew. She looked away. "Nobody, really."

"Uh huh. Who were they?" The annoyance in his tone pulled her gaze back to him. This time, his gray eyes caught her gaze.

She touched her bottom lip with her tongue, trying to decide just what to tell him. "Hunters."

"Hunting you?"

"Yes."

"Why?" He pulled into a parking lot, nosed into a parking space, and turned off the engine.

Janelle's eyes grew wide when she looked up to see the Police Department sign over the building in front of them. "Umm. Thanks for the ride." She opened the door and started to step out.

His hand caught her left wrist and pulled her back into the SUV. As he stretched, a bronze chain glinted beneath the edge of his collar. "Not going to happen, Princess. Tell me what's going on."

For a moment, Janelle thought about taking his hand off at the wrist, then realized attacking someone on police property would not be the best idea she had today. Besides, it would get blood on her clothes. She might not be a princess in the way he meant the word, but she abhorred blood. Definitely not a common trait among her kind.

She swallowed hard and took the time to glance around. Even here, the cats would attack. They were not concerned about human witnesses as her Alpha taught her to be.

3

Seeing only normal human traffic and movement in the area, she sniffed to be sure. Finally feeling safe, at least for the moment, she settled back into the bucket seat and looked at him. The impatience in his face was reflected by the thumb again tapping the steering wheel.

"Tell me why I shouldn't drag you inside for an interrogation."

Her right eyebrow quirked. *Insolence or concern?* she wondered. She slowly, but firmly, pulled her wrist from his grasp. Hands folded in her lap, she bowed her head for a long, slow breath, then tilted her head to look at him. "Who are you?"

"Kind of late to ask, isn't it?" He pulled his wallet from his jacket pocket and flashed a badge at her. "Detective Nate Rollins, San Antonio PD. Now, who are you, and what's going on?"

Janelle bowed her head again. *Wonderful. All the cars in San Antonio and I had to choose a cop's car.*

*****

Nate Rollins studied the quiet blonde. With her head bowed, her long hair the color of the full moon on a clear night obscured her face. The slender hands in her lap were white-knuckled as if she was trying to still the fine tremors he felt when he caught her wrist. She was terrified, and he wasn't letting her go until he knew why.

"I have to go," she finally said. "They'll be after me." She bit her lip as if she realized that probably

4

wasn't the thing to say to a cop.

"Who are they? Why are they after you?" He tried to infuse patience and concern into his voice and was rewarded by a quick glance from her gorgeous blue eyes. Mentally, he slapped the side of his head. *Yes, she's gorgeous,* he told himself, *but she's in trouble, so cut it out.*

"You wouldn't believe me, even if I could tell you. Please, just let me go." Her soft fingers touched the back of his right hand. "You can't help me, and they will kill you if you try."

"I believe they'll try. I want to help you, anyway." He grinned his crooked grin at her, the one his buddies called the 'lady-killer.' Not that it did him any good. He just wasn't interested in the women he knew, but it sure seemed to help when questioning female suspects. "Let's go inside, and I'll make up a report."

"No! It'll just put you all in danger. They don't care who you are. If you're helping me . . .."

"I'm not going to let you go without some answers."

Janelle sighed. She studied his eyes for a moment. He knew when she decided to trust him. Her expression changed. Not much, but enough. "Not here. Everyone you know is in danger if we stay here."

Nate frowned. The precinct was probably the safest place in town. If she was right, and the men after her were that dangerous . . .. "If you don't start talking, I'm going to drag you inside and put you into protective custody."

"You couldn't, even if you tried." She reached out and caught his wrist, just as he had done earlier to her. "Try to get loose."

He chuckled and pulled his hand. Her grasp tightened, and he felt the bones squeezed, tighter than a frail-looking woman should be able to grip. He blinked and jerked hard. Still, he couldn't get loose. He felt sweat bead his forehead. His eyes narrowed, and his jaw ticked. Even using his other hand, he couldn't pull loose from her hold. When her clutch tightened, he forced himself to relax. "Okay," he said, striving to keep the pain of her vice grip around his arm from his voice. "You can let go, now."

She released him. He whooshed out a breath and stared at the red fingermarks around his wrist. He stroked his arm and could feel the indentations she left in his flesh. "How'd you do that?"

She sucked her bottom lip between her teeth and nibbled for a second. Finally, when he thought she would refuse to answer, he heard her whisper, "I'm not human, Detective."

Chapter 2

Janelle watched the play of emotions on his face. First, disbelief, then denial, then after he looked again at the fingermarks on his wrist, a slow acceptance. She felt her face pale at his stare and swallowed. "I'm sorry. I'll leave, now."

He reached to catch her arm, but when she frowned, he stopped just before he touched her and raised both hands, palms toward her. "Wait." He cleared his throat. "I don't understand. What do you mean, 'not human?'"

She glanced around and saw some officers watching. "Please put your hands down," she murmured.

Nodding, he lowered his hands to the steering wheel. His right thumb began to tap a rapid beat before he suddenly stilled it. "Okay. I'm calm." He swallowed again, then rubbed the back of his neck. "I don't understand. Please explain what you mean."

Janelle ran both hands, fingers splayed, through her hair, and twisted it up off her neck. She wished she had something to secure it. The heat was almost unbearable. Right hand still holding her hair up, she sighed. "If you'll drive me somewhere else, I'll try to answer your questions. But," she stopped and gave him a warning look, "if you're caught with me, they will try to kill you. And likely succeed."

He met her gaze for a long moment, then nodded. Turning the ignition key, he backed out of the parking space, and then drove to the exit. Stopping at the stop sign, he glanced at her. "Mind telling me where we're going?"

"I don't know," she said, then shrugged. "Turn left and go to the Interstate. Some of my people are in Oklahoma. They may take me in."

"Oklahoma? That's at least six hours from here."

'She nodded, and let her hair drop. "They're the closest. The next closest are in Arkansas or Colorado. You can drop me off, any time you're ready to go back. I'll find my way."

Even with her Lycan hearing, she couldn't quite catch the words he mumbled under his breath. "What?"

"I said, I'm not letting you go until I know you're safe." The belligerent tilt of his chin told her that was not what he said.

She felt a grin start to form on her lips and forced her lips into a straight line. *Yup, both insolence, and concern.*

Two hours later, the hum of the motor stopped, and she woke with a start when the detective touched her hand. "We're in Georgetown. I thought you might be hungry."

Blinking rapidly in the afternoon sun that streamed through her window, she sat up straight and looked around. He pulled into a sandwich shop and parked on the back side, where they couldn't be seen from the Interstate.

"I didn't intend to go to sleep."

He nodded, a frown furrowing his forehead, as well as turning the corners of his mouth down. "How long have you been running from these, uh . . . hunters?"

8

Tears filled her eyes, but she refused to let them fall. Looking at her hands, she swallowed. "I'm not sure. A day . . . maybe two." She took a deep breath and squared her shoulders. "I'm okay. Did you say something about eating? I don't have any money, and they are tracking my accounts. That's how they found me, this time."

"Okay. I'll buy, and you can owe me one, later." He unbuckled and started to get out.

"We can't stay here. They'll find us."

"We can stay long enough to take a bathroom break and grab some food. Let's go."

"You don't understand. There're children in there. If they find us here, some will be hurt, or even killed." She swallowed again, a vision of pack children torn limb from limb, their hearts torn from their chests. Shuddering, she shook her head and pushed the memories away. "Bathroom break, and then I'm gone. If you want to stay, I'll understand."

Janelle opened the SUV door and strode toward the restaurant door. She ignored him when he caught up with her and opened the door for her. Once inside, she took a right down the hall to the restroom. After freshening up a bit, she splashed water on her face. "I won't cry, again," she told herself sternly. "I won't. They're gone, and there's nothing I can do about it." After a few ragged breaths, she snatched a paper towel from the dispenser and wiped the water from her face.

Determined, she turned toward the door. She found the detective waiting for her. When she started to step around him, he gently caught her left arm. "You're exhausted, and probably starving. Let's get something to go, and you can eat in the car."

Janelle started to shake her head, then gave him a rueful grin when her stomach decided to growl. "I guess it won't hurt to get something to eat."

He nodded and led her to the counter. Both ordered sandwiches, chips, and sodas to go. He paid with cash, and they left.

After taking a sip of his soda, he glanced at her. "Will they know you are going to Oklahoma?"

Janelle nodded. "They know where the closest pack is and that I will not be safe until I reach them."

"So, they'll be looking for you on I-35. I think we'll go a more circuitous route, then." Outside of Georgetown, he took the exit for Florence and drove over the bridge. "There's a little church house out here in the middle of nowhere. We can stop there to eat."

"You've been here before."

"Yes. I have family in the area." He turned right off the highway, drove another seven miles, and pulled into the parking lot of the small, run-down church building. Again, he drove to the back of the property, to ensure passersby wouldn't notice them.

After turning off the engine, he opened the food sack and handed her a sandwich and a small bag of chips. "I hope you don't mind the calories. You look like you could use some food, so . . .." He shrugged.

Janelle grinned. "Not human, remember. My metabolism is so fast I actually need the extra calories."

Unwrapping her sandwich, she took a bite and enjoyed the melding flavors of the cheeses and sandwich meats. For several minutes, there was no discussion. When she reached the bottom of her soda, slurping the last bit through the straw, she heard him clear his throat. She looked up to find his gaze on her.

"Okay, now that you are awake and not starving, it's time to tell me what is going on. If not . . . I'm driving to the nearest PD for help."

She rattled the ice in her soda cup, set it in the console cup holder, and turned to face him. His left thumb started thumping the steering wheel again. With a pointed look at his hand, she sighed. "Please don't do that. It distracts me."

His hand stilled, and he raised his right eyebrow. "Okay. I stopped. Now, talk. Who were those two men? Why are they hunting you? Why don't you want to go to the police for protection?"

"They are ancient enemies of my people. Usually, they are no threat to us, but," she caught her breath, and forcibly controlled the tears that again threatened "They, their people, drugged my pack. While they were incapacitated, they killed them. All of them." She swallowed and felt as if she was swallowing glass. "All of them," she whispered, her throat tight. "Even the children."

The frown that creased his forehead was back. He pursed his lips as if he wasn't sure he believed her. "So, how did you get away?"

"I wasn't there." Straightening an imaginary crease in her jeans, she swallowed again. "My Alpha, I mean, my brother gave me permission to go to school. He thought it would help us if one of us had more knowledge of finance and business. I was at school when they attacked. Otherwise, I would be dead, too." Unbidden, the tears she fought for so long started trickling down her face. "All of them. Limbs torn off, hearts ripped out . . . all dead. Even the children . . .." She couldn't talk anymore. For the first time since she returned to the ranch and found her family destroyed, she sobbed, shoulders heaving, face in her hands.

Chapter 3

Nate blinked. He didn't want to believe her, but for some reason he did. Maybe it was the anguish in her sobs. Maybe it was the gun he saw in one of the men's jackets. Maybe it was the menace on their faces. He didn't know. He only knew he believed her. At least about that. About not being human? That he wasn't sure about.

He let her cry for a few minutes until her sobs eased. At first, he only intended to pat her arm, but when he touched her, she turned toward him and leaned over the console. His right arm slipped around her shoulders, and he held her. Her right hand caught the front of his shirt and held tight, as if she was afraid he, too, would be ripped away from her.

Realistically, he knew she was suffering from grief, and probably didn't even realize that she was holding him closer to her, but he couldn't deny the electric shock that zinged through him when she first leaned into him. Awkwardly, he turned in his bucket seat and patted her back with his left hand. Slowly, her sobs became less violent. When she began to gasp to catch her breath, shudders running through her slight frame, he leaned back and looked at her. The fingers of his left hand curled under her chin and lifted her face.

With her blue eyes red and swollen, and nose running, she looked human. One hundred percent human. "Okay," he said, his tone soothing, "take a deep breath, and relax. It's going to be okay."

Fire flashed in her eyes. Her back stiffened. "It's not okay. It'll never be okay, again."

"Whoa, lady, I'm not the enemy here."

She moaned, relaxed against him, and nodded her head against his shoulder. "I know. You've been nothing but kind. I just . . . I lost everyone, and all because they wanted the ranch."

"The ranch?"

"Our home. It's private and secluded, away from outsiders. They wanted to buy it, but Randal said he wouldn't sell. So, they," she shook her head. "I can't believe they killed everyone."

"Who is everyone?"

"My brother, Randal, his wife, their four kids, and everyone else that was on the ranch."

"How many people are we talking about?"

"Besides me, there were sixty people living on the ranch." She sniffed and looked at him. "You believe me?"

"I'm starting to. Are you sure they are all dead? All sixty?"

"I didn't stay around long enough to count them all. Everyone in the main house was dead. All the kids in the schoolhouse were dead, and everyone in the barn. When I smelled them coming back, I ran. And I've been running ever since."

"Smelled them?" His left brow climbed his forehead. "You could smell them?"

She nodded. "I can actually smell a lot more than you would think. My sense of smell is even a bit stronger than theirs, but their eyesight is better."

14

Nate sighed. The not human thing again. *Well, if it's all true, she's been through a lot.* "So, they aren't human, either?"

She sniffed again and shook her head. "No. They are werecats, panther shifters."

Nate held very still. *Were . . . cats?* He forced himself to breathe. "And you are?"

Janelle raised her gaze to meet his. He caught his breath at the pain he saw in her eyes. "We are Lycan."

He couldn't help it. His right brow jumped to the same level as the left. His eyes felt like they were going to bulge right out of his head. "Like werewolves?"

For a moment, he thought something was wrong with his vision. Her eyes began to glow turquoise. Her form shimmered. Her legs and arms drew up, while her face extended into a snout. He blinked several times and shook his head in disbelief. There was a beautiful white, blue-eyed wolf sitting in his passenger seat, tongue hanging out and panting. The wolf tilted her head and whined, her paw gently tapped the back of his hand, then the wolf shimmered, arms and legs elongating, while the snout smoothed back into the face of the young blonde woman who carjacked him.

He opened his mouth to speak, but nothing came out. His breathing became rapid and shallow, and he felt light-headed. *Werewolf? She's a werewolf?* Distant memories burst into his mind. Snarling growls, saliva dripping teeth, bright turquoise eyes glowing in the dark outside his window. Remembered terror seized his mind, he could hear his childhood screams as darkness closed in on him. He fought to regain control, but the shock was too great.

The last thing he saw was her hand moving to catch his face to keep him from hitting the steering wheel.

*****

Janelle caught his cheek in her hand, just before he struck his head on the steering wheel. Of all she thought might happen, him passing out hadn't crossed her mind. Sighing, she gently maneuvered him, until he was leaning against her shoulder. Since they seemed safe enough where they were, she checked that the doors were locked, and closed her eyes for a brief rest.

*****

Nate felt warmth beneath his cheek. Eyes still closed, he took a slow, deep breath. *Ummm, she smells so good.* That thought lingered for a moment, then his eyes popped open. *She?* He sat up in a sudden jerk and stared at the sleeping woman in the seat beside him. The memory of her changing into a beautiful white wolf drifted into his thoughts, then darker, more terrifying memories invaded. Again, he could faintly hear the snarling growls and envision the savage teeth dripping saliva, bright turquoise eyes glowing in the dark outside his window. He swallowed twice. The memories started to fade. For years, he believed the memories to be a nightmare brought on by his father's death.

Now, he wasn't so sure.

He took a calming breath and willed the tight

16

muscles in his neck and shoulders to relax. *Okay,* he thought. *If it wasn't a nightmare, what was it?* For the first time as an adult, he purposely brought the memories to the forefront of his mind. His detective skills kicked in, and he started to analyze every second of the memory.

The wolf outside his window snarled and took a step toward his open bedroom window, then another. Sudden growls sounded from further in the yard and the advancing wolf hesitated, then jerked to the side to meet a dark form hurtling through the shadows toward it. Breath caught in his chest, the child Nate tip-toed to his window and pressed his nose against the screen. Snarls and growls filled the air. Two wolves clashed, ripping and tearing each other with teeth and claws. The fight seemed to last forever, but too soon it was over. The first wolf lay still in the moonlight. The second staggered to his feet and turned to look at Nate.

Nate caught his breath and took a step back into the deeper dark of his bedroom. The wolf whined. In the light of the moon, blood glistened blackly on his coat. He whined again, and then turned and ran around the corner of the house. He looked at the wolf lying in the yard, dark blood pooling beneath the torn neck. The wolf raised his head, snarled at Nate. Nate screamed. The wolf staggered to his feet, took a step toward Nate, then toppled back to the ground and didn't move again.

The bedroom door burst open and crashed into the wall. His mother scooped his pajama-clad body into her arms. "We have to go, Nate."

She pressed his face against her shoulder as she carried him through the house. Beneath his cheek, he could feel

17

her heart beating at a rapid pace. He squirmed in her arms, trying to get free.

"Where's Daddy?" His tremulous voice sounded tiny and weak.

"Daddy's not here," she said. "We have to go."

Nate jerked in her arms, looked over her shoulder. The wolf that attacked the first wolf lay on the kitchen floor, blood pooling beneath him. As Nate watched, the wolf shimmered, then slowly elongated. The legs became a man's arms and legs. The snout flowed back into the head until it became his father's face. "Daddy?"

His mother sobbed and rushed through the back door, barely sparing a glance at the man he knew was his father. On the way out, she snagged a keychain from the hook above the light switch. The door slammed behind them. Before the confused child knew what was going on, she buckled him into the backseat, and the car was careening down the driveway. He twisted and looked out the back glass and saw a man lying in the yard outside his bedroom window.

As his memories cleared away, Nate fingered the medallion hanging from the chain around his neck. "You must wear this always, Nate. Never take it off. It was a gift from your Daddy," he could hear his mother say.

Oddly, in all the years he wore it, no one asked about it. Not in school, college, the Marines, or the police academy. Each time, he waited for someone to tell him it wasn't regulation, and he couldn't wear it, but they never did. It was almost as if they couldn't see it.

"Daddy," he murmured, then shook his head. *What's going on?* he wanted to shout but didn't.

Instead, he looked at the blonde sitting beside him, her head slumped to the right against the window, softly snoring. Maybe, just maybe, the answer to his questions jumped into his vehicle. He slowly reached over and lifted several strands of her moonlight hair. The electric charge that zinged up his arm surprised him, but not as much as the thought that pushed into his mind.

Mine!

Chapter 4

Janelle woke with a start. She turned her face away from the window and froze. The detective was gently caressing her hair between his thumb and fingers. She saw the realization that she was awake in his eyes, watched his eyes widen as he dropped her hair and leaned back into his seat. As he moved, his shirt collar gaped open. Gasping, she reached inside his collar, snatched the medallion resting on his chest, pulled it out of his shirt, and held it up, pulling him toward her with the chain.

"Where did you get that?" she demanded.

His face stiffened into a stubborn glare. His right hand closed over hers. "Let it go."

For a long moment, she continued to hold the medallion. Then, as his fingers tightened, she let it go. He wasn't hurting her, but there was definite distress in his expression. "Okay. I let it go. Where did you get it?"

When he didn't release her hand, she tugged it out of his grasp.

He studied her face, then turned and put both hands on the steering wheel, as if he couldn't control them if he didn't have something to hold on to. "It was my dad's. He gave it to me not long before he died."

"You dad died? How? When?"

"You ask a lot of questions."

She sighed and turned to look out at the cactus-laden

pasture behind the old church building. It was obvious that he didn't want to discuss the medallion, but she had to know how he had a royal medallion. Very few of her kind even knew what they were, and only the Royals had them. With the medallion, she could escape the cats. They wouldn't be able to sense her at all. It would remove her *were* abilities, but it might keep her alive long enough to get to the Adair pack in Oklahoma.

"It's a . . . a special medallion. There were only ever five created. Only a few people have ever even seen one. There was one like that at the ranch when I was very small, but it disappeared. I never knew what happened to it. It only works for a small group of Lycans; most others don't even know they exist."

"But you do." He sucked air through his teeth and tilted his head. "So, what is it, if it's so special?"

Janelle swallowed. "Centuries ago, a Royal Alpha hired a witch to make five special medallions." At the mention of a witch, he harrumphed.

"You asked. I'm trying to tell you."

"Okay," he said, throwing both hands in the air in a gesture of surrender, then placing them back on the steering wheel. "I'm listening."

"The Alpha gave one each to the four Royal brothers, his heirs, then knowing it would be difficult for them to live together since all were Alpha, he sent them and their families and those who wished to join them out to start new packs." She glanced at the medallion resting on his chest and swallowed. "One of the brothers moved to China. One moved to Africa. One moved to Italy. No one knows where the fourth moved. He was never heard from again. In time, the old Alpha died. His youngest son, born after the others left, became pack Alpha, and inherited his medallion."

She picked up her soda cup from lunch and swirled it. The ice had melted. After a quick sip of the oddly flavored water, she set the cup back in the cup holder. It was too warm to be good, but wet enough to help anyway. "The youngest son was my ancestor. Eventually, old Europe became too dangerous for *were*. When the Americas opened for colonization, the pack moved here. After generations, the pack split into four: one in Arkansas, one in Colorado, one in Texas, and one in Oklahoma. We are all distant kin but don't often have much to do with one another. My pack retained the alpha's medallion, but years ago, it was lost."

Janelle turned and leaned back against the door. "Your turn. You said it was your father's, and he died. How did he die? Why did he have the medallion? Where's your mother?"

"You know witches aren't real, right?"

"Neither are werewolves, according to people who don't know better."

He grimaced and scratched his ear. "So, you really expect me to believe this medallion has some kind of magical properties?"

"I didn't say that, but, yes, it does. It is an alpha's medallion. When a direct descendant of one of the five sons wears it, he, or she, can pass for human. Other *were* can't sense him. Even other Royal *were* have trouble identifying him as *were*. Legend says if he wears the medallion before he shifts for the first time,

22

he has the same strengths and weaknesses as any normal human man, and he can't hear his wolf. Or if he does, it seems to be his own thoughts."

"His wolf." Nate shook his head. "I don't understand."

"I think you would if you took the medallion off."

"What?"

"The medallion is also spelled to prevent normal humans from touching it. It causes blisters or hives to anyone, not of Royal descent."

Nate laughed. "I've been wearing it for more than twenty years, and I have never had blisters or hives."

"That's the point." With tentative fingers, she reached out to touch the medallion. He twitched but sat still when she picked it up. "If you take this off, I think you will find that you, too, are Lycan. When I first smelled you, there was something familiar in your scent. You don't smell human, but you don't smell *were*, either. That's why I chose you."

"You can smell *were*?" Fingers splayed, he ran his left hand through his hair.

She nodded. "What happened to your father, Detective?"

"Nate."

"What?"

"My name is Nate." His thumb started tapping the steering wheel.

Janelle gently covered his hand with hers. "That is difficult for *were* to handle. It makes me want to pounce."

Nate sat very still. "Pounce."

"Yes. Fast, jerky movements make me want to attack. I'm an adult, so I can control the urge, but it isn't easy.

23

Please don't do that."

He blew out his breath through puffed cheeks. "My dad always hated that, too." He sucked his lips between his teeth. After a moment, he gave her a cocky grin. "So, you're telling me I'm a werewolf? And I'm just supposed to believe you with no proof?"

"The proof is in the medallion. Remove it, and you will know either way." She released the metal and let it fall to his chest. "I won't touch it, while you have it off."

Again, he studied her. "If I'm *were*, and I take it off, what happens?"

"I'm not really sure. Since you have never shifted, at your age, you might experience some discomfort. The first time is usually a little painful, but it doesn't last long. After you've practiced for a while, it doesn't hurt, anymore."

"It's still daylight, and there won't be a full moon for days, yet."

Janelle laughed. "The full moon thing isn't what you think it is. Yes, the urge is stronger during the full moon, but you can change any time you want to. If you have Royal blood, and I think you do, you will still have clothes on when you shift back. If not, they will rip off you when you change. It takes a lot of training for non-royals to maintain control of their clothing as well as their physical bodies."

"So, just take the medallion off, then what?"

"Then you'll hear your wolf, and you will be able to shift."

"Hear my wolf?" He shook his head, frowning. "I

don't understand."

"It's really hard to explain. Your wolf is part of you. It's as if you are two beings in one; one human, one wild wolf. You usually can't control the wolf, he won't let you, but, you can become friends with him, partners. Only the strongest of Alphas can force their will on their wolf." Janelle glanced around to make sure no one had found them. "It might be a good idea to get out of the car, first. If you truly are Lycan, you may not be able to control the first shift. You wouldn't want to tear up the upholstery."

*****

Nate shook his head. "I think you're nuts."

"Maybe. What do you have to lose?"

He fingered the bronze medallion for a moment. He could almost hear his mother warning him to never take it off. She reinforced the instructions with her last breath. "Always wear your father's medallion, Nate. It will keep you safe."

Safe from what? he asked, but she wouldn't rest until he agreed. To make her happy, he nodded. An hour later, she took a final breath and died. *I've always worn it. Always. But if Janelle's right . . ..*

Coming to a decision, he opened his door and stepped out into the early afternoon. A cool breeze feathered through his hair. When he heard her door open, he turned and looked at her across the top of the SUV. "Just take it off?"

She nodded. "Set it on top of the car." She sniffed several times, then nodded again.

25

He raised his eyebrow. "Smell something?"

"No, nothing important. There's nothing to fear here. You can take it off without worry."

Nate clutched the medallion for a moment, then whipped the chain over his head. He looked at it for several long moments, then heaved a long, shaky sigh and set it on the top of his SUV.

"Now what?" he asked, then doubled over in pain. *Free!* "Ahhh! What's happening?"

Janelle walked around the vehicle and dropped to her knees in front of him. She caught both his shoulders. "Look at me." She shook him. "Look at me!"

Eyes glazed with agony, he looked into her eyes. *Mine!* reverberated through his mind. *Mine!*

He moaned as he felt his body quiver and wrench into an unaccustomed form. The pain felt as if it would last forever. Finally, it faded away. Whining, he licked his lips and nuzzled her face. The wolf took control. Pushing her to the ground, he straddled her body, his face nose-to-nose with hers. *Mine!*

Her eyes widened in surprise. Her head turned to the side, offering her neck to him . . . acknowledging his Alpha power. He licked her neck. It was all Nate could do not to bite, make her his, but he forced the wolf back. In his mind, he heard the wolf whine, not knowing what else to do, he mentally stroked the wolf's head like he would a large dog. *It's okay,* he told the wolf. *We'll figure this out together.* Slowly, he backed off her and sat on his haunches by the SUV door. He shook his head and swiped his nose with his paw. *How,* he

26

wondered, *do I change back?* The wolf whined again, and Nate realized the wolf didn't know, either.

Chapter 5

Without taking her gaze off Nate, Janelle slowly sat up and brushed the leaves and dirt off her elbows and arms. As wolves go, he was magnificent. Taller than normal, with deep blue-black fur and gray eyes. She had been sure he was *were*, but his strong Alpha presence left her rattled. What flustered her most, though, was the thought that burst into her mind from his, *Mine!* The wolf claimed her, but the man did not. For some reason, the bite she expected never came. Janelle didn't know whether to be grateful or resentful.

For the first time, a wolf wanted her wolf. The man obviously didn't but instead fought his wolf off. Otherwise, the wolf would have laid claim. She swallowed. *I'll deal with that, later*, she thought. Head tilted, she watched him. Suddenly, she realized his problem. "You can't shift back, can you?"

The wolf shook his massive head, confirming her thought. He whined, walked to her, and rested his massive head on her lap, looking up at her. He watched her tentative reach toward him but did nothing when she gently ran her fingers through the fur between his ears. She gazed into his turquoise eyes and felt her wolf's interest.

"To turn back," she said, her voice soft and soothing, "you must think about being human: how it feels to have your longer legs and arms, how it feels to talk, how it feels to move. Close your eyes, and think

28

about those things. Get it clear in your mind, and you will shift."

Those gray eyes held steady, watching her. The wolf wagged his tail and licked her hand. She could feel the internal struggle Nate fought with his wolf. The wolf's muscles were tense under her stroking hands. She bit her lip, then thought, *Nate, can you hear me?*

The wolf growled softly, and Janelle laughed. "So, you aren't pleased with him, huh, big guy?" She caught the wolf's head in her hands and raised his face so she could see in his eyes. "You have to let him shift back for this to be settled."

The wolf wiggled, withdrew his head from her hands, and caught her left hand in his teeth, firmly, but not breaking the skin. He pulled her to her feet, then backed up until they were standing by the SUV. Releasing her hand, he jumped up on the side of the SUV and looked at the medallion, then looked at her. With a soft whine, he tilted his head and looked from her to the medallion.

"Oh!" Janelle snatched the medallion and draped it around the wolf's neck. "Is that what you wanted?"

The wolf yelped and dropped to all four feet. He shimmered, legs and arms elongating, body reforming into that of a man, and snout smoothly flowing into the detective's face. Nate fell forward against her legs, then leaned back against the SUV. Expression tight with pain, he looked up at her.

"Ouch," was all he said.

Janelle couldn't help it; she laughed. "Do you need help up?" she asked, holding her hand out to him.

He caught her hand and pulled himself up, head bowed.

29

Her hand still in his, he cleared his throat and looked at her from the corner of his eye. "I think we need to talk."

Janelle nodded and swallowed. *He really doesn't want the bond his wolf wants,* she thought. Again, she didn't know how to process that thought. It hurt in some ways, but in some ways, she was thankful she wasn't forced into a relationship she didn't know for sure she wanted. As a Royal descendant, she'd always known that she would be taken as mate to a powerful wolf. That she would be spurned never occurred to her.

*****

Nate raised his hand and studied her smaller hand inside his grasp. He blew out his breath through puffed cheeks. *Mine!* the wolf insisted.

You don't know that, Nate thought. *She has the right to choose.* Nate could feel the bewilderment his wolf felt.

With a sigh, he dropped her hand and raised his gaze to her eyes. "I don't know much about being a werewolf. I've read a lot. Always been fascinated by the topic, because of some things I saw when I was a kid, but never believed in them. Not really. I thought my memories were just nightmares." He shook his head and laughed. "I don't think I really wanted to believe in them."

"And now?"

"My wolf . . .."

"What's his name?"

"What?"

"What's your wolf's name? My wolf is Nadrai. Who is your wolf?"

Nate blinked at her for a moment. "I . . . don't know."

"So, ask him."

Ask him, she says. I suppose I could. Nate turned his attention to the wolf he felt pacing inside him. *What is your name?*

I am Koreth.

"He says his name is Koreth."

She nodded. "Nadrai and I are happy to meet you, Koreth."

Koreth preened, and Nate got the distinct feeling he was a bit proud of himself. A grin quirked his lip. "He said he is glad to meet his one." He shrugged. "I'm not really sure what he means."

Janelle covered her mouth with both hands. She didn't laugh out loud, but merriment danced in her eyes. "You really don't understand, do you?"

"No. And I don't understand why I can feel him, now, but couldn't before."

"Have you always worn the medallion?"

"Since I was about five years old. Why?"

"*Were* don't fully come into their wolves until puberty. If you've worn the medallion that long, he never had the chance to break out. You just went through what most of us go through in our early teens." She stopped and looked at him, solemn. "I hope you can adjust because now that he has been released, you won't be able to imprison him again. While you wear the medallion, other *were* won't be able to sense you or him, and you won't have the same abilities you will have without the medallion, such as strength and sense of smell. Your wolf, however, will still be present and able to sense things around you. His abilities will give you a small bit of extra protection."

"I think there is a lot I need to learn, but . . .." Nate broke off when his cell phone rang. He glanced at the caller id and shook his head. "My captain. I'm on vacation, so I'm not sure why he would call."

I don't like him. He smells like cat. Nate could hear Koreth growling but realized Janelle could not hear Koreth.

"Why can't you hear Koreth, too?"

She sent an annoyed look at the phone. "I can when you're in wolf form, but not when you're in man form. Only mated wolves can hear each other in both forms."

"Mated?" Nate flicked the Ignore button and replaced the cell in the dashboard bin.

Mine! A growl accompanied the thought this time.

Fingers splayed, Nate ran his left hand through his hair. "My wolf keeps saying, mine. I don't suppose you know what that means? I mean, I think I know what he means, but . . .."

Janelle grinned. "But . . .."

Nate felt heat flood into his face. "I think he means that he wants you, um, your wolf, as a mate."

The amusement in her expression vanished. "But you aren't interested."

At her flat tone, Nate tilted his head to the side and studied her as she started to turn away. "I didn't say that."

Chapter 6

Captain Benjamin Garrett slammed down the phone, muttering an expletive. He spun around to face the two men sprawled in chairs opposite his desk. "He isn't answering."

Wiping his face with his left hand, he sat so hard his desk chair rolled back a few inches. "You're sure this," he held up a scrap of paper with a license plate number written on it, "is the license of the car she got into?"

The blonde man nodded. "She jumped in his vehicle, and he sped off. We just barely got the plate number before they were gone."

The captain frowned. "Officer Ramirez saw Detective Rollins pull into the lot with a blonde woman. They seemed to be arguing, then they left."

The other man leaned forward, expression intense and threatening. "Under the circumstances, either he's helping her, or she kidnapped him."

Garrett sighed. "I don't like this. Rollins is my best detective. I don't want anything to happen to him, even if I don't like him personally."

"You don't like him?" asked the blonde.

"No, Martin, I don't like him. He smells off. Not *were*, just . . . off. It keeps me off kilter when he's around."

Martin jumped to his feet and stalked back and forth across the office. "Well, we have to find him. He can lead us to the girl. We can't let her get to Oklahoma. If she contacts the Were Council, we could lose everything we have gained."

"You'll lose more than that. If the Council gets involved, your life is forfeit after all you and your cats have done."

Martin stopped in front of the desk and leaned over it, both hands flat on the wooden desktop. "That's why you're going to help us. Find out where they are. We'll take care of it from there." Behind Martin, Franklin, his second, stared at Garrett., eyes full of menace.

Garrett ignored Franklin and tried to match Martin's stare, but couldn't. Martin was the Queen's Tom. In the human world, Garrett had power. In the *were* world, his power meant nothing. Sighing, he picked up his phone. "Jenson, we have reason to believe that Rollins has been kidnapped by a woman the FBI are after. See if you can locate his cell phone for me." He listened for a moment, then said, "I know it's not regulation, but if he isn't in trouble, I don't want to put him there. Find out where he is and let me know." He listened again, then said. "Thanks."

Garrett hung up the phone and looked at Martin. Several minutes later, Garrett answered his phone on the first ring, listened to Jenson's report. He said, "Thanks, Jenson," then hung up.

"His phone is in Williamson County, somewhere between Georgetown and Florence."

Martin stood straight. "I would hate to think you would inform him that we are coming."

Shaking his head, Garrett sighed. "I wouldn't dare."

34

Chapter 7

Janelle started to turn away, but his words stopped her. Hands trembling, she faced him. The embarrassment on his face was almost funny. Almost. She hesitated, measuring him for a moment. "Then why stop Koreth? Why not let him make claim?"

"Just like that? I don't know you. You don't know me." He shook his head. "I couldn't let that happen. How would it be different than rape?"

Janelle felt her mouth drop open. *Rape?* The idea never occurred to her. It was so foreign to the way *were* thought, that she didn't know how to respond. Even her brother would have considered it normal. She tried several times to speak, but couldn't find words. Finally, she huffed and leaned against the SUV. A moment later, she started laughing.

Nate jammed his hands in his jean pockets. "What's so funny?"

"You are." She struggled to get control. Sucking her lips between her teeth, she tightened her jaws. Clearing her throat, she regained her composure, then said, "You said your dad died. Was that before you were given the medallion?"

He shook his head. "He gave me the medallion a few days before he died. Mom and I moved to Texas. She remarried when I was ten and died of cancer just before my twelfth birthday. Her last request was that I never take the medallion off, and I haven't. Until today."

"Your step-father?"

His face froze into blankness. "I don't know where he is. He dropped me off at an ice cream parlor and never returned." His look dared her to feel sorry for him. "When he couldn't be found, I was sent into foster care."

Warily, she eyed him. The friendly man she had been with was suddenly withdrawn. "I . . .." She stopped and sniffed, then sniffed again. "Cats!"

She turned to run, but his hand caught her and pulled her back. "Get in the car."

"But . . .."

Nate pulled her around to the passenger's side, jerked the door open, and shoved her inside. "Buckle up."

Without quite intending to, Janelle found the belt and snapped the buckle. Nate opened his door and slid in beside her. Biting her lip, Janelle watched him lock the doors. "They'll kill you if they catch us!" she said.

"They won't catch us, and if they do . . .." His buckle clicked, then the motor roared to life. "My spare gun is in the glove box. Get it out." Gravel flew as he threw the SUV into gear and hit the accelerator. As he sped around the old church building a black panther ran at the front of his SUV. Rather than slow down or turn, Nate gave the car more gas and sped toward the panther. At the last moment, the panther leaped to the side, claws scraping the full length of the vehicle as they sped past.

He glanced at her and frowned. "Where is my gun?"

"I don't like guns."

"Get it out, anyway."

Janelle fumbled with the glove box and pulled out Nate's gun. Face wrinkled with distaste, she moved her cup and dropped the gun, barrel first, into the cup holder. With nothing else to do with her drink, she slurped the warm liquid through the straw, then dropped the empty cup into the back floorboard.

Another panther raced across the church parking lot and jumped on the hood of the car. Janelle screamed when a massive paw slammed into the windshield. A crack streaked across the full width of the window. Nate slammed on the brakes, causing the panther to tumble off the hood. He immediately pressed the accelerator to the floor. The SUV bumped and rocked as he ran over the panther. Without reducing speed more than necessary, he turned on the old country road and sped into the country.

Nate glanced in the rearview mirror. "One down."

"Not really."

He flashed a look at her, then turned back to the road. "What do you mean?"

"Unless you rupture the brain, the spinal cord, or the heart, *were* rejuvenate."

"Rejuvenate? As in heal?"

"As in heal very, very quickly."

Nate muttered an expletive under his breath. "How did they find us?"

"I don't know. They have someone who can access computer records at the bank, or they wouldn't have found me so quick after I used my debit card. Maybe they have someone who could find your SUV through the DMV?"

"They have hackers that good?"

"I just don't know."

Nate sped around a curve and slammed to a stop at the Stop sign on Highway 190. A glance in the mirror told him the cats had been left behind, at least temporarily. "You said they know you are going to Oklahoma?"

"Yes."

He looked both directions; the highway was empty. Nate turned left and started back toward the Interstate. Within seconds, he was pushing eighty miles-per-hour, then pushed the speed even higher. Instead of crossing the bridge and heading north on I-35, he turned right on the access road toward Georgetown. At the first entrance ramp, he pulled onto I-35 heading south.

"Where are we going? Oklahoma is the other direction."

"I know." Nate glanced in the rearview mirror. So far, none of the cars behind him appeared threatening. "They expect you to go north, so we are going south."

Chapter 8

Captain Garrett picked up the phone. "Garrett here."

"We lost them. See if you can locate them."

"How could you lose them?"

A growl came over the phone. "Your man is good." There was a pause. "You sure he's human?"

"I've never had reason to think otherwise." Garrett wiped his face with his broad hand. "I'll see what I can find out."

"The girl had a gun."

"He a hostage?"

"Use that as a basis to find out where they are."

Garrett sighed his frustration. "Call back in a few minutes."

Martin grunted and hung up.

This was shaping up to be bad business all the way around. Either Rollins was helping the girl, or he was a hostage. Either way, he was unlikely to live through being found by the cats. As a lone cat, Martin was not his Tom. Technically, he didn't have to obey his demands. Technically. *But if Martin wins, and I go against him, I'll be on his hit list. And I don't really like Rollins.* Garrett stepped out from behind his massive wooden desk and paced his small office. No, he didn't like Rollins, but then it wasn't his job to like the men who worked for him. Sending assassins after one of them grated.

After several minutes, he picked up the phone and dialed Rollins' cell phone. Again, no answer. Reaching into his pocket, he pulled out his personal cell and tapped in a quick text. *Now, it's up to Nate.*

*****

When Nate's phone rang, he glanced at the caller id. His captain again. Nate frowned and swiped the ignore button. He never talked on the phone while driving. Seconds later, his phone dinged. He could see the message was from Garrett. Sighing, he handed the phone to Janelle.

"Read that to me."

Janelle took the phone. Her eyes grew wide as she read aloud, "Nate, call me immediately. Emergency. You and the girl will die if you don't call."

Nate glanced at her, took in her pale face and the teeth chewing her bottom lip. With a muttered curse, he glanced in the rearview mirror to verify the cats hadn't caught up with them and whipped to the side of the road. Foot on the brake, SUV still in gear to enable a quick departure, he took the phone from Janelle's trembling fingers and tapped the call button next to his captain's name.

"Rollins, where are you?" Garrett's voice sounded strained.

"On vacation. What's up?"

"The girl still with you?"

"What girl?"

He heard Garrett take a deep breath. "Rollins, there are assassins looking for her. You're in danger as long as you're with her."

40

Nate frowned. "Are you suggesting I abandon her?"

He heard another sigh. "No, I'm telling you they have access to police and bank records. If you're going to live through this, you must go off-grid. Get rid of the phone. Don't use your cards. Find a different vehicle. And keep your eyes open."

Nate's left eyebrow climbed up his forehead. "Where are you getting your information?" At the back of his mind, he heard his wolf snarl, *Cat!*

"Just get rid of the phone, or they'll know where you are again."

"Panthers just attacked me." Nate heard a sharp, indrawn breath over the phone. "What do you know about that?"

"You wouldn't believe me. Just go off-grid. Now. Call me back from a pay phone or get a burner and call." Garrett hung up.

After a glance at Janelle, Nate popped open the back of his phone and pulled the battery and the SIM card. He rolled the passenger window down and handed her the phone. "Toss it as far as you can."

Janelle took the phone and threw it as hard as she could into the center of a clump of prickly pear cactus on the other side of the pasture fence. While she discarded the phone, Nate took the pocket knife from his left front pocket and cut the SIM card in half. He gave her half of the SIM and she threw it across the pasture fence, too.

Checking for traffic, he waited until it was clear, and pulled out on the interstate. A half mile down the road, he handed the battery and the rest of the SIM card to her. Without a word, she tossed both out the open window, then rolled the window up.

"What are we going to do?"

Nate's wolf swaggered at the trust in her voice. Pursing his lips, Nate glanced at her, then turned his attention back to the road ahead. "You don't have any money?"

"No."

He nodded. "They already know we're in this area. I'll stop in Georgetown and pull as much as I can from my account." He sucked air through his front teeth. "Where is this ranch you told me about?"

"What?"

"The ranch. They wouldn't expect you to go back there. Where is it?"

"South and east of Austin."

He nodded. "That's where we're going."

*****

The phone rang. Garrett stared at it for several seconds, dreading the call. After four rings, he picked it up. "Garrett, here."

"So, where are they?"

"I don't know. They've gone off-grid. We can't get a lock on his cell location."

There was an ominous silence on the line. After long enervating seconds, Martin's voice continued. "Put out an APB."

Garrett sighed. "On what grounds?"

"Kidnapping."

Not for the first time, Garrett wished he never met

Martin and his henchman. "You have to come in and swear out a complaint for that."

Again, there was silence on the line. "If I find out you are helping them . . .."

"I'm not crazy," said Garrett as emotionless as he could. "But I have to follow the rules. I can't issue an all points without a charge."

Muttered cursing came over the phone, then the call ended.

Garrett wiped the sweat from his face and stared at the phone cradled in his hand. "What have I done?" he whispered.

Chapter 9

Nate pulled into a parking spot at a Georgetown bank. He slipped the gun under his seat, then glanced at Janelle. "Let's go."

"The last time I used my card, they found me."

He frowned at the shiver that ran through her small frame. "Did they somehow put a hold on your accounts?"

"I don't think so."

He nodded. "We don't know how long we have to go off-grid. Use your card to get as much as you can in cash. I'll do the same. That way we will have money for gas and food while we figure out what to do."

Her blue eyes studied him for long moments, then she nodded. "Okay. Then what?"

He took a deep breath. "We go to a discount store and get a burner phone. Do you know how to contact your people in Oklahoma?"

"Yes, but I've been too busy trying to stay alive to contact them. And I left my phone at the ranch."

"Will they help?"

Janelle considered his question for a moment, then nodded. "I think so. While there is even one member of a pack alive, the property belongs to the pack. If we all die, the Were Council will award the property to whatever *were* group is in the area." Turquoise glowed briefly in her eyes. He watched her struggle with the effort to remain in human form. When her eyes were again a deep ocean blue, her face set hard in anger, she said, "That's why they have to kill me. Until I die, they can't legally get their hands on the ranch. If they proceed, and I show up, the Council will destroy their clowder."

"Clowder?"

"That's what a group of werecats is called."

"Okay. We'll get all the cash we can. Then, we get a phone and start trying to contact the Council." He stopped as a tear rolled down her pale cheek. With one finger, he caught the tear and lifted it from her face. She caught her breath when he touched her. He wanted so much to pull her into his arms and kiss her. "I can't bring back what you've lost, but I will help you keep what remains." He knew that without the medallion, he wouldn't be able to control the angry beast pacing within. "Koreth promises this, also."

Janelle nodded, her gaze captured by his. When he reached up and gently wiped the tears from her eyes with his thumbs, she leaned into his hands. Koreth growled. Nate could feel the wolf's frustration. He wanted Nadrai as his mate. Nate wanted to kiss Janelle, but . . ..

Janelle pressed her lips against his in a brief kiss, then pulled away. Startled, Nate watched as she got out of the car and waited for him to join her in the parking lot. He blew out a breath through puffed cheeks. A glance at his watch told him he better hurry or the bank would close. Deciding to put off thinking about her kiss, he got out and walked around to stand next to her.

He held his hand toward her, uncertain of her reaction. When she caught his hand in hers, Koreth's thought was smug. *Mine.* There was no demand. Just a statement of

45

fact.

*****

An hour later, after emptying and closing his account, Nate drove down the SH130 toll road toward Seguin. He hoped the cats would keep searching along I-35, while he and Janelle made good time in a different direction. With less traffic on the toll road, he knew it would be easier to spot the cats if they did catch up to them.

He reached over and stroked Janelle's face with the back of his fingers, waking her, then gripped the steering wheel again. "We're coming up on Seguin. You need to stop for anything?"

She sat up straighter, cleared her throat, and blinked at him. "What? Oh, no. I don't need to stop." When he glanced at her, her face reddened. "Sorry for sleeping, again."

"No problem. How long have you been awake? I mean before you jumped in my SUV?"

"Um, two, maybe three days. I'm not sure, now. It all kind of blurs together."

"Sorry to wake you, but you said I needed to get off 130 around Seguin, and we're just about there."

Janelle folded her arms bent over her head, hands clasped, and leaned back in a cramped stretch. "Take the I-10 exit," she said through a yawn, "then take I-10 east."

A while later, Nate eased into I-10 traffic. From there, she directed him to Hallettsville, then to a farm

46

to market road to the ranch. The closer they came to their destination, the more agitated Janelle became. "Will they be at the ranch?" asked Nate.

"I don't know."

"Is there a back way to the ranch?"

"Yes, drive past the entrance about ten miles and take a left on the country road just past a bend in the road. The back entrance is a bit over eighteen miles from the front entrance."

He nodded. "That's what we will do, then. No point in advertising our presence."

"You could drive on to town, and pick up something to eat and some camping equipment if you wanted to."

Nate's eyebrow quirked. "Werewolves need camping equipment?"

Embarrassment showed on her red cheeks. "Well, no, not as wolves, but I wasn't sure you wanted to change again."

"What do werewolves eat, when they are, uh, wolves? Please don't tell me you eat dog food." Koreth growled at him, while Janelle laughed.

"No. Wolves hunt, if they are hungry. Whatever they find to eat, it sustains us, too."

Nate wrinkled his nose. "Maybe we should get some supplies. I'm not ready to eat raw meat." His left thumb tapped the steering wheel absently until Janelle cleared her throat. "Oh, sorry. I forgot." He grinned at her. "While we are there, let's get a burner phone, too. I think we both need to make some calls."

Chapter 10

Two hours later, shopping all done, Nate stopped at the back gate at the ranch. Janelle jumped out, tapped the security code into the lock, opened the gate, waited for him to drive through, then shut and locked the gate. She climbed in and pointed ahead. "There is a split in the road about a half mile from here. Go left. The road to the right goes back to the main compound."

With a nod, Nate pressed the accelerator. "Is there a good place to camp out here?"

"We should probably stay away from the line shack, but there is a cave on the other side of it, down a long and unused dirt road."

Nate took the left road, driving slow. He didn't want to raise a cloud of dust for any cats present on the ranch to see. When he topped a low hill and could see an old, run-down house, he stopped. "Is that the line shack?"

Janelle nodded and rolled her window down. "Turn off the engine for a minute." When the engine cut off, she leaned out the window, listening and sniffing the air. After several minutes, she pulled back into the vehicle. "I don't smell any cats around here. If they were in the line shack, I think I would know."

"Ready to go, then?"

"Yes. On the other side of the shack, there is a faint road to the left. The cave will be about two miles after we turn."

"Okay." Nate started the car and headed toward the

shack. He missed the dirt road, it was so grown over with weeds. Janelle pointed it out, and he backed up, then turned onto it. Not only was it overgrown, there were places that had washed out, leaving deep ruts in the road. Long before they arrived at the cave, Nate was glad he was driving an SUV.

He stopped at the end of the road and looked at Janelle. She was putting the battery in the burner phone they purchased. Nate reached under his seat for his gun, slipped it into his jacket pocket, then opened his door and started around the back of the SUV to start unloading their supplies. Just as he got to the back of the vehicle, he heard a low, threatening growl. In his mind, he heard Koreth give a warning growl. Hands out to the side, Nate turned to face a young gray wolf.

"Janelle, I think you have a friend out here!"

When he called, Janelle looked in the mirror and saw the wolf growling threats at Nate. She jerked the door open and tried to bail out, before remembering her seat belt was still buckled. Muttering, she snapped the lock and jumped out. She ran to the back of the SUV and dropped to her knees. "Ayden!"

Threatening growls instantly changed to welcoming barks. The young wolf threw himself into Janelle's arms, whining and licking her face. After petting him and stroking the gray fur behind his ears, she leaned back. "It's okay, Ayden. You can shift."

The wolf glanced at Nate, then looked back at Janelle. At her nod, he stepped back, then shimmered, transforming into a teenager. Evidently, he was not a royal. Nate opened the back of the SUV, pulled out a pair

49

of sweats, and handed them to the boy.

Reese, Ayden's human, made short work of pulling them on. "Who is he?"

"He's a friend, and he is helping us." Janelle grabbed his shoulders and turned him to face her. "How did you get away? Are there any others?"

Reese nodded. "We were on a training run when the cats came. It was over before we got back, so we hid here in the caves until we could decide what to do."

"I thought you were all dead." Janelle swallowed a sob and blinked to keep tears from falling. "How many are here?"

"Twelve. The two older classes. Jonathan is here, too, but the cats hurt him. We think they had silver on their claws because he isn't healing."

"Take us to him."

"Him, too?"

"Yes, him, too. It's a long story, but he is on our side."

The boy sighed. "They're in the cave. I was standing guard." He turned and led them into the trees. They soon came to a small, gurgling stream, and splashed through it. The cave was behind brush on the opposite side of the stream. Reese held the brush aside so they could enter the low opening.

Nate waved Janelle to enter first. He didn't want to startle frightened wolves into attacking before she was there to stop them. She snickered at him as she bent low to enter the cave. Once inside, Nate's eyes adjusted to the dimmer light. He counted six teens and four young wolves sitting on boulders around a small fire circle.

Back against the cave wall, a man who appeared about Nate's age raised up on his elbow.

"Janelle," he said, "I saw them chasing you. I couldn't get up, so I couldn't help you. How did you get away?"

"I ran them through the outer trap. One of them was caught, and the other stopped to save him. It gave me time to get away." She rushed to him. "I thought you were all dead, Jonathan!"

"If they hadn't gone after you, they would have gotten me, too. Reese found me and carried me outside the compound. As soon as it was dark, he brought me and the rest of the kids to the caves." He leaned back, his face tight with pain. "We've been here ever since. I was sure they would find us by now, but Reese tells me there were only the four cats. They've all been gone since the attack."

Janelle nodded. "They've been searching for me. Two of them found me in San Antonio, and would have caught me, except that I car-jacked some help."

For the first time, his gaze went past Janelle to Nate. His eyes narrowed, and a low growl came from his throat. Janelle put a hand on his shoulder. "It's okay. He's with me."

The moment her hand touched Jonathan's shoulder, Nate growled. Janelle turned to look at Nate and saw him looking at her hand on Jonathan's shoulder. "He's a friend, Nate. And he's hurt. And he thinks you might be a threat."

Nate realized that Koreth was pushing his feelings through him and struggled to control the possessiveness Koreth felt. He swallowed, swallowed again, and then in a tight voice said, "I think it would help if you took your hand off him."

"Oh!" Janelle jerked her hand away from Jonathan's shoulder. She stood and faced Nate. "Sorry. I didn't think."

"What's going on?" asked Jonathan.

Before Janelle could answer, Nate stepped closer. "Koreth has claimed Nadrai as his mate. He isn't happy Janelle is touching you."

"Koreth?"

Nate and Janelle looked at each other, then both sighed at the same time. "My wolf," said Nate, his tone flat.

"You're a wolf?" asked Jonathan. "You don't smell wolf.

"I am."

"Koreth claimed Nadrai?" Jonathan blinked. "You didn't claim Janelle?"

Janelle looked down, almost as if she were ashamed. Nate frowned. He took another two steps, curled his fingers under her chin and raised her face to see her eyes. "Why are you embarrassed?"

"You didn't want me."

"I already told you, that's not true. I just wanted to give you time to make up your own mind. I won't force you into something you don't want or are not ready for."

Her gaze searched Nate's face as if she looked for answers to her questions. "I never once thought I would have a choice. I was taught that when my wolf was claimed, I would be mate to the man." She swallowed. "Nadrai is attracted to Koreth. I . . .." She cleared her throat and glanced at the interested faces of the teens

52

and wolves watching them. "I do not object."

Nate studied her face for a few more seconds before tilting his head and giving her his 'lady-killer' grin. "Then I will claim you, Janelle." He lowered his voice and leaned closer. "But I don't know how."

Snickers and laughs sounded around him. Eyebrows raised, he looked around the cave. Janelle laughed. "Wolf hearing. You might as well not have whispered. I'll explain everything later. Right now, we have to see what we can do to help Jonathan." She caught Nate's face in both her hands. "Koreth, I have to touch him to help him. Nate will protect me. Jonathan will not try to claim me. Right, Jonathan?"

"Uh, yeah. I won't try to claim you." He snorted. "You're like a kid sister to me, Janelle."

"I know that, but Nate and Koreth don't."

Nate nodded. "Koreth says okay, but make it fast."

Janelle laughed. "Will do, big guy."

Chapter 11

After taking a quick look at Jonathan's wounds, Janelle decided she needed more light. She, Nate, Reese, and two other teens went to the SUV and unloaded the camp supplies they purchased. Janelle set up a small camp table, set two small LCD lamps on it, and switched them on. Nate unfolded one of the camp stools, then helped Jonathan onto it, so Janelle could more easily see the scratches on his chest and side. Jonathan was not steady, so Nate stood behind him, supporting him, while Janelle gently removed the tattered shirt that clung to his wounds. A sharp intake of breath was the only sound Jonathan made when Janelle pulled scabs off with the shirt. Beneath the scraps of fabric, the wounds were festering.

"Reese said they used silver on their claws? What does that mean?" asked Nate.

Janelle didn't look up from her task. "It means that the wounds won't heal unless they are cleaned properly." She dabbed at the wounds with a clean cotton towel. "Reese, do you know where to find garlic and honey?"

"There's some garlic growing along the creek, and I think there is some honey in the warehouse." He blushed. "Jonathan told me not to go after it, or I would've already treated it."

Janelle nodded. "Someone will have to go after the honey. And we need garlic. In the meantime, Lisa, take one of the wolves with you and get a pan of fresh water."

A girl Nate thought was about fifteen took the pan Janelle handed to her. One of the wolves stood and followed her out.

"The kids can't go alone to the compound," interrupted Jonathan. "If the cats come back. . .."

"I'll take Reese to show me the way and get what you need," said Nate.

Jonathan twisted enough to see Nate, grunting with pain as he moved. "They'll kill you if they can."

"They've been trying all day." Nate looked at Janelle. "You said they won't rejuvenate if they have brain, spine, or heart injuries?"

"Yes." She hesitated, licked her bottom lip. "Are you sure? You don't have all your abilities, while you wear . . . uh, while you . . .."

"Reese will have all his. He can warn me if there is trouble, right?"

Janelle nodded. "But he hasn't come into his full strength, yet. He won't be much help in a fight if the cats come."

"I don't need a babysitter or bodyguard, just a guide." Nate grinned and patted his jacket. "I have an equalizer to use if needed."

For a moment, Janelle studied him. Nate wondered if she was as concerned about him as Nadrai would be about Koreth. "We'll be okay," he finally told her. "I'll take care of him."

Janelle took a deep breath and nodded. "I know."

After Lisa and her companion brought the water, Janelle cleaned Jonathan's wounds as best she could and bandaged him using a torn shirt. Nate helped her get their patient on the new sleeping bag Janelle stretched out on the cot Jonathan was using, then clapped a hand on Reese's back. "Ready?"

Reese nodded, but Nate could see the doubt in his eyes. "I suppose so."

Nate looked at Reese for a minute, then pulled out his badge and handed it to the boy. Reese looked at it, then raised his gaze to Nate. "You're a cop?"

"Detective. This werewolf thing is a bit new to me, but I have lots of training through the PD Academy and the U.S. Marines. Koreth and I won't let anything happen to you."

"Marines, huh?" The boy took a deep breath and handed back the badge. "I don't understand how this is new to you."

"It's a long story, and one I'll be happy to share. But right now, we need to get those supplies and more food. Janelle and I didn't bring enough for everyone."

Reese looked at Janelle. "You really trust him?"

"Yes. He saved me from the cats, twice. You can count on him." She quirked a grin at Nate. "I trust him."

"Okay." Reese walked to the mouth of the cave and motioned for Nate to follow. "Let's go."

*****

Since they needed to gather supplies, Nate decided to take the SUV, rather than walk to the ranch compound. It took almost an hour, driving slow enough to prevent dust rising to give them away, and driving a circuitous route to make sure the cats wouldn't realize they came from the direction of the cave if they were discovered.

It was almost dark by the time the main house came into view. Nate braked to a stop, rolled the windows down, and turned off the motor. Just as Janelle had done much earlier in the day, Reese leaned out the window and sniffed the air. After a bit, he lowered himself back into the car and shook his head.

"All I can smell is death. I guess the cats just left everyone where they died." He swallowed, and Nate looked away to give the boy time to regain control of his emotions.

"Let's leave the SUV here, then, and walk in. That way maybe you can hear them before they come at us if they are here."

Reese nodded. Soon they were pressed up against the side of the main house, both looking for movement in the compound yard. Nate could see bodies lying in the grass between the houses and barn. A quick glance told him tears streamed down Reese's face, but the boy was alert.

Nate kept his voice soft. "Where is the warehouse?"

"On the other side of the barn."

"Okay. Let's go the long way around, rather than go straight there."

The boy nodded again.

Nate led the way around the back of the main house, then skirted behind two more houses. The barn was ahead; another building was off to the right. "Is that it?"

"Yes."

"Follow me." Nate stepped out into the open. He

stopped for a minute to study the area and check for movement, then quickly walked across the open area. When he reached the warehouse, he pressed his back against the wall and turned to watch Reese's back as he followed. Reese tilted his head to the left, so Nate moved in that direction alongside the building until he came to a corner, glanced around, then rushed to the warehouse door. Reese crowded in behind him and shut the door. Before Nate's eyes adjusted to the darkness inside, Reese snapped the light switch. Florescent lights flashed on, illuminating the room.

For a moment, Nate considered telling him to shut off the lights, then realized that they needed the lights to find everything. He followed Reese further into the building. Reese grabbed a crate and started filling it with nonperishable food. Before Nate could remind him of the honey, he saw Reese set two quarts of honey in the crate. While Reese filled the crate with supplies and started on another, Nate looked around. There was an area with medical supplies, including bandages and ointments. Nate grabbed an armful of gauze bandages, ointments, and painkillers, and dumped them into the crates around the other supplies.

"About done, Reese?"

"I think I have everything Janelle listed." Reese took two blankets from the shelf and tucked one each over the crate contents to keep them in place.

"Okay. Let's go to the door. We're going to turn off the lights and open the door from the side. Before we go out, I want you to see if you can smell anything to be concerned about."

Reese nodded. They carried the two crates to the door and set them down. Nate signaled Reese, and he switched off the lights. After their eyes adjusted to the darkness, Reese opened the door. Nate took out his Glock. If there was anything waiting for them, he wanted to be ready. Reese stood to the side of the open door and sniffed.

"I don't think there are any cats out there, but it's really hard to tell with all the . . . um, smells."

"Okay. Can you carry both crates?"

"I think so." Reese's eyes narrowed. "Why?"

"Not all the way to the car, just until I know we don't have company." Nate waggled his gun where Reese could see it. "I can't shoot if I have a crate in my hands."

"Oh. Sure, I can carry them."

Nate helped Reese balance a crate on each hip. "Let's go, then."

Nate stepped out first, searching the shadows for furtive movements. Seeing none, he motioned for Reese to follow. This time, rather than skulk, he decided a direct route made more sense. He walked quickly across the center of the lawn to the road where the SUV was parked. Reese, one crate under each arm, followed. As they passed several bodies, Reese sobbed once, then was quiet. Nate glanced back at the boy and saw him walking with his eyes closed. He stopped and waited until Reese caught up with him.

"You have to help me watch, Reese. I know it's hard, but I can't do this alone."

Reese nodded, started to say something, then his eyes grew wide with fear. He seemed to be frozen. Nate turned to face the threat behind him. A black panther snarled and leaped at him. Nate brought the pistol up, snapped a shot. When the cat fell from the air, Nate took his time and put a bullet in the feline's brain.

"Look out!" Reese dropped the crates and gave Nate a shove. Another cat missed Nate, struck Reese in the chest and they hit the ground rolling. Snarls and shouts filled the air. Nate tried to line up his Glock to take a shot but was afraid he would hit Reese.

With a muttered curse, Nate shoved the gun into his pocket and ripped the chain from around his neck. By the time the cat realized he had a much larger, more powerful adversary, Koreth's jaws clamped around the cat's neck, yanking him away from Reese.

Chapter 12

As soon as the cat was pulled off, Reese shifted, his clothes ripping during the change. His wolf jumped into the fray, hamstringing the cat's left hind leg. Between the two wolves, the cat fought a losing battle. Reese's wolf staggered away from the fallen cat and changed back to human. Claw marks scored his chest and arms, while his face sported teeth marks. The teeth marks started rapidly healing, but the claw marks did not.

Koreth gave the panther one last savage shake, then dropped him and turned to study Reese. He walked over to the medallion Nate dropped, picked it up in his teeth, and carried it to Reese. Koreth put the medallion on the ground by Reese's foot, tapped it with a paw, and whined, head tilted to the left.

Reese swallowed. Koreth was the largest wolf he had ever seen. At first, he didn't understand what Koreth wanted, but when the older wolf tapped the medallion again, Reese nodded. Moaning with the effort of stretching to pick up the medallion, he lifted it. After looking at it for a moment, he draped the chain around Koreth's neck.

Koreth shimmered. Nate appeared when the shimmering stopped, still in his jeans and jacket. After shuddering, Nate reached into his jacket and removed his pistol. With no mercy in his expression, he turned and walked to the cat. He lowered himself to a squat and waited until the panther shimmered into the form of a man, then tapped his gun barrel against the man's face.

"Who are you?"

The man, one of the two who had been chasing Janelle, snarled at him. "You'll die when the clowder arrives."

Nate studied the man, watching as his wounds visibly healed. "Not too worried about that." Again, he tapped the man's face with his gun. "I asked you a question. Who are you? Why did you do this?" He motioned toward the dead.

"The better question is 'who are you?' And why can't I smell dog on you?"

Koreth growled in Nate's mind. Nate tilted his head, his gaze boring into the werecat. Maybe he had watched too many movies. He couldn't resist. He shrugged. "I'm your worst nightmare."

Behind him, he heard Reese snicker. "I'm also an impatient man. Who are you? What are you doing here? Why kill all these people? What do you hope to gain? How many of you are there?"

"My name is Martin." Martin laughed. "You're a dead man. I'm not telling you anything else."

Nate nodded, his mouth drawn thin in displeasure. "I kind of figured you'd say something like that." He leaned back on his heels, his gun still held casually. "That woman you've been chasing is mine, so I take exception to it."

Martin snarled at him. "She won't be for long. You'll all be dead before long."

For a moment, Nate thought about his oath as a police officer. Then he thought about the atrocities he saw in the Middle East. He glanced at the bodies strewn about the compound yard. This was so much worse. Then he thought of a terrified Janelle jumping into his SUV. Nate felt Koreth's rage building and realized he, too, was furious. "Maybe. Maybe not. Either way, you won't see it." Nate moved the trajectory of his pistol and shot the cat through the right eye.

Nate's gaze was drawn to the man's hands. Silver tips were sheathed around his fingers. Nate bent forward and slipped one of the tips off. The silver was uncomfortable in his hand, but with the medallion on, it didn't burn him. He never liked silver much. Now he knew why. He slipped the silver tip into his pocket.

Walking to Reese, he dropped to sit flat, his arm draped over his raised left knee, his gun hand propped and ready. "Are you okay?" His gaze swept over the teen. "How bad are you hurt?"

Reese tried to get up and was not able to stand. He shuddered. "Not as bad as Jonathan, I think, but bad enough."

Nate nodded. "Let's get you back to the cave."

Reese shook his head. "Not without the supplies."

"I'll load it. Wait here a bit." It took a minute to gather everything back into the crates, but fortunately, nothing had broken. The gauze packages Nate shoved into each crate protected the glass bottled items.

He snatched one of the blankets Reese tucked around the top of the crates and handed it to Reese. Reese gasped as he moved enough to wrap the blanket around himself. Nate raised an eyebrow at the words Reese muttered, but he knew the boy was hurting and kept his thoughts to himself.

After loading the two crates in the SUV, Nate carried the wounded teen to the vehicle and set him into the passenger seat. Before he got into the SUV, he went back to look at the two dead men. The other man was the second that had been chasing Janelle when she jumped into his car. In his mind, Koreth growled at the two men. Nate shook his head and walked back to the car. If these were the only two involved, it was over. But Jonathan said there were four, and Martin said more were coming . . ..

Nate started the car, spun in reverse, slammed the gear into drive and sped back to the cave to get medical treatment for the teen passed out in his passenger seat. He drove as close to the cave as he could. When he pulled up outside the cave, he stepped out and shouted for Janelle.

Janelle slipped out of the cave and splashed through the creek as she ran to the SUV. Ignoring her wet shoes, she arrived just as Nate opened the passenger door. "What happened to Reese? You were supposed to protect him!"

Nate slipped his arms around the teen and lifted him from the SUV. "There were two of them."

Reese in his arms, he turned and faced the anger in Janelle's expression. "He's alive. They aren't."

Janelle's eyes widened. "You killed them?"

"I didn't have much choice. It was the same two who were after you. I couldn't let them hurt you, and they were determined to kill you. All of us, really."

She ran her fingers through her moonlight colored

hair and shook her head. The anger in her expression didn't fade. Her lips were compressed. She was trying, Nate thought, to keep from saying something they would both regret. Finally, she jerked her head toward the cave entrance. "Bring him in and let me see how bad it is."

Chapter 13

The next morning, after sitting up nursing both her patients all night long, Janelle slumped in the camp chair Nate set up for her the night before. She dozed, dreaming of being chased by cats until she heard Reese whisper her name. Startled, she sat up, blinked several times, then when she realized her dreams were only dreams, she leaned toward Reese and brushed the hair out of his eyes.

"How do you feel," she asked softly, trying not to wake the others.

"Like a cat clawed my ribs," Reese whispered through a tight grin.

Janelle smiled. "You'll be okay. After I cleaned your cuts and scratches, I applied a garlic and honey ointment. The scratches are already healing. The cuts will take a little longer."

He laughed, then caught his breath and winced. "Guess I won't have to worry about vampires for a while."

"Nope. Not for a while. Do you need anything?"

Reese caught Janelle's hand. "Have you seen his wolf?"

"Nate's? Koreth?"

"Yeah. He's huge. I've never seen a wolf that big."

Janelle nodded. "He's a Royal." For a moment, the anger she felt for Nate allowing Reese to be hurt must have shown on her face.

"Don't be mad at him, Janelle." Reese raised up on his elbow. Sweat popped out on his brow, and his breathing was labored. "If not for him, I would be dead. He shifted and pulled the cat off me."

"But he should have prevented . . .."

"There was so much death in the air, I didn't smell them. When I saw the first one, he was sneaking up on Nate. I froze, but Nate shot him out of the air. Then the second one jumped at him, but I pushed him out of the way and the cat got me, instead." The boy's face was earnest. "Nate tried to question one of them, but the cat wouldn't answer. He just kept threatening you, so Nate shot him. Jonathan or I would have done the same thing."

Janelle stroked his forehead. It hurt to see one of the young wolves injured. Unbidden, her first sight of the pups in the compound school room rushed to her mind. Fighting tears she didn't want to shed in front of Reese, she sighed. "So, you think a lot of him, huh?"

"If he wants to be Alpha, he has my vote."

Janelle laughed. Reese was too young to vote on such things, but it was impressive that Nate won his loyalty. Reese was a loner and seldom wanted much to do with pack business. Of course, it might just be that he was still a kid. *Was a kid. He's growing up too fast. They all are.* Janelle sighed.

She glanced at the teens and wolves resting around the fire circle, then looked at Nate. Nate sat on his heels close to the cave entrance, back leaned against the cave wall. His pistol was in his hand. If anything, or anyone, came into the cave, she had no doubt that Nate would take care of it. She sighed again. "Maybe I will cut him some slack," she murmured to Reese. "He's doing pretty well, considering he didn't even know he was *were* until yesterday."

"What?"

"Did you see his medallion?"

Reese nodded, and slowly leaned back until he was stretched out. "I've never seen one like it before. Koreth brought it to me. He didn't shift until I put it on him."

"It's bewitched. While he wears it, other *were* can't feel him or smell that he is *were*. He is basically human while wearing it. It's an ancient talisman given to only five Royal brothers. All he knows is it was his father's. Nate's father died before he went through puberty, and he's worn the medallion since he was five, so he didn't know he was *were* until yesterday."

"Wow. Must have been quite a shock."

Janelle looked at Reese for a moment, then turned and looked at Nate's sleeping form. "Yes, I suppose it was." She watched Nate for a few minutes, then turned back to Reese. "You, pup, need more sleep. Shut your eyes for a while longer."

Reese grinned at her, then obediently closed his eyes. Janelle glanced from Reese back to Nate. Nadrai nudged her mind. *He is a good wolf. A good mate.* Janelle nodded. *I think you are right, Nadrai.*

*****

The brush at the cave mouth rustled. All the teens and all three adults jerked to wakefulness. A muttered

68

curse preceded a balding man into the cave. He came to an abrupt stop, hands in the air when he saw the Glock aimed at his face. "No need for that, Rollins. I just wanted to make sure you were still alive."

Cat! growled Koreth.

"Cat," one of the girls called out. Instantly, there were ten wolves in the cave. The only four who didn't shift were the adults and Reese.

Garrett glanced at the wolves, stiff with hackles raised, growling at him. He swallowed, then wide-eyed, turned back to Nate. "I'm not here to cause trouble. I just wanted to make sure you were okay."

Nate ignored the kids. He kept the gun aimed at Garrett. "Why should I believe you?"

"I warned you. I told you to go off-grid."

"You knew they were after us?"

Garrett cleared his throat. "They came to me to find you. All they had was a license number."

Nate felt Koreth growling, the threat even more palpable than that from the kids. Nate mentally stroked the wolf. *Wait*, he commanded. Koreth settled on his haunches, but Nate knew it wouldn't take much for him to push to take over. He wasn't at all sure that Koreth couldn't push past the medallion's effects. "You told them where we were."

"The first time." He glanced at the growling wolves that inched closer. "They didn't tell me what they did at the ranch until later. I didn't know they intended to kill you, until then, either. Martin is the Queen's Tom, Nate. You don't understand that, but I couldn't stop him. That's why I called you. I waited until I figured you had gone off-

69

grid before I had Jenkins try to find your phone. That way, I could tell Martin I couldn't help him find you."

"So, why did you help us?

Garret shook his head. "You're one of my best men. How can I let an outsider take one of mine?"

Nate studied him for a moment, then nodded. He holstered the gun, then motioned for the kids to back up. "He's okay."

"He's a cat, Nate."

"I heard, Janelle, but he helped us. If he hadn't, we probably wouldn't have made it back to the ranch." With a glance at Garrett, he asked. "Are there more cats here?"

"Not yet." Garrett waved his hands. "May I?"

"Uh, yeah, you can put your hands down. Just know this, Captain, if you threaten or try to hurt anyone here, I'll put a bullet in your head."

"Duly noted." He looked at the wolves, then back at Nate. "I'm surprised you have taken all this so well. Most people can't accept *were*."

"He's . . .." began Reese.

Nate threw Reese a warning look and interrupted the teen. "Let's just say, I don't surprise easily."

"I knew that about you. That's why you're actually the best man in my squad." He turned his attention to the two resting on cots and frowned. "Don't wolves heal as fast as panthers do?"

"They do," said Janelle, "if they aren't poisoned with silver."

The shock that splashed across Garrett's face could not have been faked. "Silver? Do you have medicine?"

70

"I cleaned it with fresh water, then used garlic and honey ointment."

Garrett nodded. "That should be a good remedy. How long ago were they wounded?"

"Reese was wounded last night. It's been several days for Jonathan."

Janelle cast a worried glance at Jonathan.

"I take it Reese is almost healed, but Jonathan is still infected." The captain wiped his face with his left hand, sighed, and turned to Nate. "Do you trust me?"

"Maybe."

"I can help your friend, but I'll need some wild onion and some goldenseal."

Nate stared at him for a minute, then nodded. "How much? Where do I find it?"

"About a handful of goldenseal flowers and roots, and as much onion as you can hold in your hand. I need the dirt around the onion roots, too. Both should be growing close to the creek outside."

"I'll get it," said Janelle. "Nate can stay here to keep an eye on you."

Garrett sighed. "I wouldn't expect anything else." He looked at Nate from the corner of his eye. "I'll need a pot of water, too."

Nate glanced at one of the older wolves. Nate still didn't know most of their names, so he just nodded at one of them. The wolf shimmered into a human boy. The teen was wearing jeans, so Nate knew from Janelle's explanation that he had been trained to control his clothing. The boy picked up an empty cookpot, bent low, and followed Janelle out the cave mouth. While Janelle and the boy were gone, Nate motioned toward an empty camp chair. "Have a seat." It wasn't so much to make Garrett comfortable as it was to have more control. From the look Garrett threw at him before sitting, he knew exactly what Nate was thinking.

Chapter 14

An hour later, Garrett stirred a bubbling concoction over a wire rack placed over the small fire in the fire circle. He tapped the wooden spoon on the edge, then used a towel to lift the hot pot off the rack and set it on a large flat stone several feet from the fire circle. "It should be ready."

Jonathan wrinkled his nose. "I'm not drinking that. It smells to high heaven."

Garrett laughed. "You don't have to drink it. We will soak bandages in it, then wrap your wounds."

"How does it work? Magic?" Janelle looked dubious.

"That's a good question," said Nate. "How do we know you aren't poisoning him. The other cats used poison."

"I'm not one of them. I'm a lone tom. I haven't been part of a clowder in more than forty years."

"Why?"

Garrett opened one of the boxes of gauze bandages and dropped the gauze in the mixture he cooked. "My mate was killed by a rival." He shredded the empty box in his hands. "Rather than take another, I renounced my position as second in my clowder and left."

"And your rival?" asked Jonathan.

Garrett shook his head in refusal. Nate realized they wouldn't learn more about his rival.

Janelle cleared her throat. "Why are you helping us?"

"The clowder Queen is bitter, greedy, covetous of anything other's own, including your ranch." With a glance at Nate, Garrett continued, "I spent a few years living with a witch out in Nebraska after I left the clowder." He motioned toward the potion he made. "I learned some healing craft from her. I don't think there is any magic in this, just the herbs, but I'm not sure. I do know it works, even for silver-contaminated wounds."

Nate turned to Janelle. "I think we can trust him. Go ahead and use it to doctor Jonathan's wounds."

"Are you sure?" Distaste wrinkled her nose, much as Jonathan's did. "It smells like medicine, but . . .."

"But because a lone tom gave it to you, you will let your pack mate suffer?" Garrett shook his head. "Okay, I'll tell you something no panther should ever tell wolves. Nate, silver doesn't affect cats the way it does wolves. That's why they can use it without fearing to poison themselves. To poison cats, you use a combination of catnip and foxglove."

Both Nate's eyebrows arched high. "Did you know that, Janelle?"

"No."

"So, why would you tell us how to poison you, Garrett?"

"First, I don't believe you would, Nate. Second, you may need the information when the clowder shows up."

Garrett had the full attention of all the wolves, human and canine. Nate glanced around the circle, then leaned toward Garrett. "When are they coming?"

"That I don't know. I do know that Martin was the clowder Queen's tom." He stopped and cast his gaze toward Nate. "I'm assuming Martin is dead."

Nate pursed his lips and tilted his head, but did not verbally answer Garrett.

"I figured as much when I found you alive." After scratching the side of his head, Garrett wiped the sweat from his face with his large hand. "I didn't go to the ranch compound, but after what Martin told me, this must be all that are alive." He motioned to the group around him.

"Greed killed my mate. Greed killed all of your family and friends," Garrett said to Janelle. "Maybe I don't owe you anything, but I want to stop Lorena. I have a score to settle with the queen."

"They will mark you a traitor," said Jonathan. "You'll be on their hit list, too."

"There's been enough unnecessary and unprovoked death." He turned to look at the entire group. "I didn't know they were going to do this. Had I, I would have tried to stop it. I'll do anything I can to keep the rest of you alive." Garrett turned to face Nate. "I'll even swear allegiance to the pack, if necessary."

"Allegiance to the pack?" Nate looked at Janelle, then past her at Jonathan. "I'm not sure I know just what that means."

"It means that he would become a part of the pack, adopted in if he is accepted," said Jonathan, his face expressionless. "It doesn't happen often."

After several seconds of silence that Nate thought must be unnerving to Garrett, Jonathan cleared his throat. "The Alpha would decide that."

"The Alpha." Nate sighed. "The Alpha died at the compound."

Jonathan winced as he sat up on the cot. "We have a

new Alpha."

"You do?" Nate quirked an eyebrow at Janelle. "I don't know how that kind of thing is decided. Who is it? You, Jonathan?"

"No, not Jonathan," said Janelle. She walked over to Nate and dropped to her knees in front of him. All the wolves shimmered to human. As one, they, too, dropped to their knees. "You are our Alpha, Nate. We have selected you."

"A human?" Garrett shook his head. His strangled expression was almost funny. "You want a human to be pack Alpha?"

Nate ignored Garrett. Koreth was radiating pride, fiercely happy to be the pack Alpha. *I don't know how,* Nate thought to Koreth. *We will do this together,* Koreth told him. Koreth was wagging his tail. *We are Alpha!* Nate looked from Janelle to each of the kneeling teens, then looked at Jonathan. "Me?"

Jonathan nodded. "I'm Beta, Nate. Always have been. I'll do anything in my ability to protect the pack and help in any way I can, but I'm not Alpha. I can't do it. None of the kids is old enough or experienced enough in dealing with the dangers ahead. You haven't said, but I can see you have military training. We need you."

A wide grin filled Reese's face. "He's a Marine. He told me so."

Janelle smiled and looked up at Nate. "You can refuse, but you are the chosen Alpha."

Nate sighed and ran both hands through his hair. "If you are sure."

76

Garrett harrumphed. "Never heard of a human Alpha."

Leaning over, Nate took Janelle's elbow and lifted her to her feet. After looking a silent question at her, and receiving a grin and nod in return, Nate took off the medallion and gave it to her. *That didn't even hurt that time,* he thought to Koreth after the shift. Koreth grinned a wolfy grin and looked at Garrett. *I am Alpha, cat. I accept your allegiance. Should you betray it, your life is forfeit.*

Wordless, Garrett dropped to his knees and bowed his head. A moment later, a black panther shimmered into existence before the Alpha. *I give you my oath of allegiance, Alpha.*

Chapter 15

Squatting on the creek bank, Nate tossed a twig into the swiftly flowing creek. Koreth heard Garrett's quiet footsteps behind him and warned Nate. *Would have been nice to have these enhanced senses in Iraq,* Nate thought to Koreth. Until Garrett's soft voice intruded on his thoughts, Nate ignored him.

"I think we should talk."

"Uh huh." Nate snapped his wrist and watched another twig splash. "Have a sit."

Garrett sat on the rock next to Nate, feet hanging inches above the flowing water.

After several minutes, Nate turned to look at him. "Something in particular on your mind?"

"How long have you known?"

"Found out yesterday when your buddies were chasing us." Nate almost grinned at the discomfort he saw on his boss' face.

"They weren't my buddies, Nate." Garrett wiped his face. "I left the clowder a long time ago, but if I had been there, I would have tried to stop the attack."

Nate nodded. "I believe you." He turned full-on to study his captain. "The question is, what will they do now. Do they know some of us survived?"

Garrett shook his head. "I honestly don't know. Probably not. Martin wanted to remain tom to the Queen, so I don't think he would have admitted to failure. He was pretty insistent on catching the girl before the clowder or the council found out she was alive."

"So, they didn't know the kids were alive, either." Nate sighed. "Makes sense. If they had, they would have hunted them down, too."

"Even though they are almost grown, they would have been no match for Martin and Franklin. Those two were combat experts. Their mistake was to take you for a normal person. They didn't think even a cop would give them trouble. Their tactics would have been different had they known you are *were*."

With a sigh, Nate glanced back at the brush-covered cave mouth. "We can't stay here. Do you have any idea when the rest will show up?"

"It's hard to say. I think they'll wait for a while, waiting for Martin to call with the all-clear. Eventually, when he doesn't, they'll either send someone to check or come en masse." Garrett cleared his throat. "Your vacation is up on Monday. You coming back to work?"

Nate sucked air through his teeth. "Not sure, yet. You off the entire weekend?"

Garrett nodded. "I have some time built up, though, if you want me to stay here and help."

"Why? I mean, why did you offer allegiance? I wouldn't have let them hurt you."

"I know. It's just . . . I'm tired of being alone, and I don't want to be part of a clowder that would do what these cats have done. Too many years as a cop, I guess."

"You're too close to retirement to give that up, Garrett."

"Maybe."

Nate's left thumb started tapping his knee. When he

noticed Garrett watching it, he stopped. "Cats have trouble with jerky movements, too?"

"Yeah." Garrett studied the creek bed for a moment, then grinned at Nate. "That trait always drove me mad."

Nate laughed. "I thought so. That's one reason I kept doing it." He laughed again at the startled look Garrett threw at him. "Just one way to put it to the man in charge, you know."

Garrett chuckled. "Guess it's my turn to figure out what will put it to you."

Nate grinned. "I look forward to it." After looking at the sky for a moment, Nate stood up. "Best be deciding what to do. We have dead to bury." He shook his head. "I don't even know what rituals wolves have for their dead. It needs to be taken care of, though. Let's go."

When Nate entered the cave, Garrett right behind him, he found Janelle helping Jonathan sit up. "Better?" Nate asked.

Jonathan winced and nodded. "Almost healed. Garrett's potion seems to have helped." He glanced down at the bandages wrapped around his torso, then shrugged. "Think I'll always have scars, though."

Garrett nodded. "Too much time passed for the wounds to heal invisibly."

"At least they are healing." Janelle steadied Jonathan while he slipped on a shirt. She grinned at him. "Some of the ladies will think it is attractive."

Nate growled, startling himself as much as it did Janelle. Janelle laughed at him. "Take it easy, big boy.

I didn't mean me."

Mine. Nate shook his head. "Koreth doesn't like you teasing like that, Janelle."

Jonathan nodded. "It will be better once you have properly claimed your mate, but Koreth will never like her teasing another wolf."

"I'm sorry." She almost looked contrite.

Koreth was mollified, but Nate could see the impishness dancing in her eyes. He sighed and shook his head. Learning the ins and outs of pack life was going to be interesting. "I think we need to make some plans."

Immediately, all the teens gathered and sat in a circle around him. Janelle, Jonathan, and Garrett also sat facing him. Nate blew out a breath. "It's going to take me a while to get used to this." His hand swept out to include them all. "So, you're going to have to be patient with me, till I figure it all out."

The group nodded. Their solemn expressions made Nate a bit uncomfortable. "First, we need to decide what to do about the dead on the ranch. I don't know anything about death rituals for wolves, so I'll need some guidance on that." He quirked an eyebrow at the group. "Anyone?"

"The dead are usually cremated, Nate. We mourn while they become ashes to replenish the forest of our home."

"Individually? Or is it permissible to have a mass cremation?"

Tears slipped down Janelle's face. "Under the circumstances, with the threat we face, perhaps a mass cremation is the best idea."

Nate glanced at each of the faces before him, giving even the youngest wolf the opportunity to nod acceptance to Janelle's plan. "Okay. Jonathan, how soon will you be up and around?"

"A few more hours should do it."

"Reese?"

"I'm fine, now. Just a little sore." The boy stretched to prove he could move well enough to be useful.

"Alright. Reese, Garrett, Jonathan, and . . .." Nate looked at the other teens, then pointed at one of the boys who seemed to be older than the others. "You. What is your name?"

"Bobby."

"Reese, Garrett, Jonathan, Bobbie and I will gather the bodies and start the preparations for the cremation." He looked at Janelle. "You and the rest can start cleaning up the houses and buildings."

Janelle blanched but nodded.

"Something wrong?"

"I . . . I hate blood." She swallowed with difficulty, then raised her head to meet his gaze. "But I will do it, Nate."

Nate studied her for a moment, then nodded. "Today, we all have to do things we don't want to do." His gentle voice seemed to calm her nerves, and she nodded, her expression tight.

"Garrett, what are you driving?"

"My pick up. The quad cab."

"Okay, Jonathan, you ride in the truck with Garrett. Reese is in the SUV with me and Janelle. Those who can't fit inside the vehicles will ride in the truck bed. Bobby, you ride up front with Jonathan and Garrett."

At Bobby's startled look, Nate quirked his eyebrow.

"Problem?"

Face pale, Bobby shook his head.

"Let's go, then, wolves." After a quick glance at Garrett, Nate grinned. "Or cats, if it fits better."

Chapter 16

When the group arrived at the edge of the compound clearing, Nate pulled off the road and braked the SUV. Garrett parked behind him. They all debarked from the vehicles and Nate waited for everyone to gather round. While waiting, Nate studied the compound grounds. Nothing seemed to have changed.

"Okay." He turned back to the pack. "Janelle, keep your group together. Stay here until I call you in. No one goes anywhere alone. Those with me, we'll start with the bodies in the yard, then clean out the main house. After we get them all out, Janelle, your group will go in and start cleaning up in there, while we start on the other buildings. I want one person on each team wolfed to keep watch while the others are working."

Garrett shuffled his feet in the dry Texas dirt road. "What about the dead cats?"

Nate looked at Garrett. "I don't know how the cats deal with their dead."

"They usually bury their dead."

Nate pursed his lips and considered Garrett. "You can dig a grave for them up on the hill if you wish."

Garrett looked relieved. "I would like that. I didn't care for them, but . . . .."

Nate raised a hand to stop him. "I won't hold a service for them."

"Understandable." Garrett studied his shoes for a moment. "I'll take care of everything for those two."

"Okay, then, let's get to work."

"Hey," said Reese. "What's that?" He walked over to a canister on the ground and picked it up. After turning it over in his hands, he held it to his nose and started to sniff.

Garrett knocked it out of his hand. "Don't!" When Reese started to growl at him, Garrett raised both hands and bowed his head.

"Hold it, Reese." Nate stepped between the two. As soon as Reese bowed his head in submission, Nate turned to Garrett. "What are you doing?"

"That's poison. It's probably what they used in the attack."

Nate walked to the canister and picked it up. Rather than sniff it, he turned it, looking for writing. "I don't see anything."

"You wouldn't. The clowder uses them to control vermin. Unlike werewolves, our kittens are born with the ability to shift. Because the kittens are too young to understand training, the clowder doesn't allow them to chase mice or other small animals. So, they use these bombs to poison the small creatures while the kittens are in the field. Before they are brought back home, the mice and other small animals have been disposed of."

Nate's eyes narrowed, and he frowned. "So, we are talking premeditated murder. Jonathan, do we have a map of the ranch?"

Jonathan cleared his throat and nodded. "There's one in the house."

"Good. Okay, guys, Jonathan is going to get the map and a marker. We will tack it to the barn door. These canisters are evidence of a crime. When you find the

canisters, I want them brought and put them in . . .."
Nate stopped and glanced around the yard. Finally, he
located a small wooden crate up against the side of the
barn. "Put them in that crate. Then use the marker to
note on the map exactly where you found them. Be sure
you wash your hands after handling these things."

As the first order of business, they spread out
searching for the poison canisters. Six of the poison
bombs were found and their locations marked on the
map. Over the next four hours, Nate's team carried the
bodies of the pack into a shallow ditch, then began
working on a low, wide bonfire for the cremation. Once
the bodies were arranged on the bier branches, Nate
walked to the main house. He crossed the wide porch,
opened the door and stepped in.

All the drapes and curtains had been taken down
from the windows and all cloth upholstered furniture
removed. The ceilings, walls, and floors throughout the
house had been scrubbed, as well as the rest of the
furnishings, but Nate knew that the bloodstains would
still be visible with fluorescein.

"Janelle?"

"In the kitchen."

Nate followed her voice down a long hall and
stepped into a bright, antiseptic-smelling room. Here,
too, all the curtains had been taken from the windows.
Soon the walls and ceilings would have to be painted,
and the floors recovered to completely rid the house of
the smell of blood. For a moment, he wondered if it
would be better to destroy the house and rebuild. He
shook his head and put that thought aside for a later

time.

Janelle finished wiping the marble counter, tossed the dishcloth into the sink, and turned to face Nate. "I think the house is as good as we can get it."

Nate studied her pale face and her trembling hands. He could tell she really, really didn't like to deal with blood. Koreth's pride in her ability to overcome her own distaste to complete the task given her washed over him, and he smiled gently at her. "We are ready for cremation. Let's get everyone to the bier. I really would like to get it done before dark."

Janelle nodded, then called her team to her. They followed him outside and across the field to the bier. Jonathan and the teens shifted and evenly circled the bier.

Garrett slipped into the circle and nodded at Nate's questioning glance. "All done."

Janelle moved into place next to Nate. Everyone turned to look at Nate. After glancing from one expectant look to another, Nate leaned closer to Janelle. "Am I missing something?"

"As Alpha, you must light the bier."

"Ah. Got any matches?"

"You shouldn't need matches, Nate. You are a Royal Alpha. Koreth will have the power to start the bier without them."

Both Nate's eyebrows jumped almost to his hairline. "Magic?"

"Of a type. Koreth will have an Alpha's abilities, including the ability to start fires."

"So just shift?"

Janelle nodded.

"Okay." He removed the medallion and set it on the ground between his feet. *It's your turn, Koreth*, thought Nate. Moments later, Koreth stood in Nate's place. Janelle shifted, too. Koreth looked at each of the others, noting their faith in him, then studied Garrett's cat. *Your name, cat?*

The panther bowed his head. *I am Marcel.*

To Nate's surprise, Koreth stood on his hind legs. *I am Alpha. As from the beginning, as unto the end.* He tapped his front paws together, then swept them in a pushing motion toward the bier. *Now from the end, return to the beginning.*

Fire burst forth from the center of the bier, burning even hotter than Nate expected the flames to be. As the fire dimmed, Koreth raised his muzzle to the sky and howled, long and mournful. Immediately, the howls of the pack wolves and the snarl of the pack panther joined him. Within minutes, the entire bier was burned to ash, the ash of the bodies mingling with the wood ash. The mourning continued until the fire burned out.

Again, Koreth tapped his front paws together and swept them toward the ash. *Return to the forest.* A swiftly whirling wind picked up the ashes and drew them high into the sky before dissipating and allowing them to float gently to trees below.

Chapter 17

Before it became dark, the teens found sheets to drape over the windows. Nate set guards for the night; Jonathan and Reese until midnight, Nate and Garrett from midnight until 4 a.m., and then Bobby and Janelle from 4 a.m. to 8 a.m., at which time Jonathan would be awake and keep watch again.

While the teen boys finished covering the windows, Janelle, Gayle, and Amelie pulled meat from the freezer and prepared spaghetti and meatballs. Paisley, Isabella, and Lisa set the table and prepared drinks.

Jonathan gave Nate and Garrett a tour of the house. When he took them upstairs, he stopped at the first door. "This is the office our pack Alpha used. It's your office, now, Nate."

When he walked in, Nate looked back at Jonathan. "This room wasn't touched by the cats?"

"No. It was locked and there was no one in here, so they had no reason to force entry." Jonathan motioned toward the desk. "We only kept it locked to keep the pups out. Randal, our previous Alpha, kept important documents in here, and didn't want the kids coloring or drawing on them."

"Documents?"

"The ranch deed, bank, stock, and investment records, as well as birth records for the pack."

Nate walked to the massive wooden desk and sat in the executive style chair. Waving a hand at the chairs facing the desk, he put his elbows on the desk and rested his chin on his clasped fingers. "Birth records." He watched as Garrett and Jonathan sat facing him. Nate glanced at Garrett, then looked at Jonathan. "I suppose we'll have to file death certificates?"

"No. We kept our own records of births and deaths. We have falsified documents for when we need to be out in the world, but there are no actual 'official' records of any of us." Jonathan frowned. "We should record the deaths that occurred and the cause of death. Since there were so many at one time, we must submit it to the Council."

"The Council." Nate looked from Jonathan to Garrett. "And they are?"

"The Council," said Garrett, "is a body of *were* representatives from many different tribes. They are what passes for law among the *were*." He sighed and shook his head. "They're not going to be happy with what's happened here. The clowder will be highly censured and, depending on how involved the Queen was in the attack, ..."

Nate raised an eyebrow in question. "What?"

Jonathan answered him. "The entire clowder could be exterminated."

"Exterminated?"

Garrett's expression was strained. He nodded. "Even the kittens."

Nate blew out a loud sigh. "Even though they had nothing to do with it?"

"Even so." A flicker of apprehension touched Garrett's face. "Especially if you, as the Alpha, demand it."

For a moment, Nate just stared at Garrett, but when he glanced at Jonathan, the beta was nodding. "As the Alpha," said Jonathan, "you have the right to demand justice for the near extermination of our pack." His expression troubled, Jonathan continued, "You also have the right to request leniency on the clowder and ask that only those involved be punished."

"And your recommendation would be . . .."

Jonathan threw his head back, eyes narrowed, face tight. "My pack was almost destroyed. They must be punished." He glared at Nate for a moment, then sighed. "At the same time, I have no desire to see kittens killed for the crimes of their elders."

"Neither have I." Nate tilted his head and clapped a hand on his captain's shoulder. "However, those responsible must be held accountable, one way or another." He felt his wolf's emotions flaring through him and shrugged. "Even if I felt differently, and I don't, Koreth would demand justice for the pack."

Garrett swallowed and wiped his face. "I agree those responsible must be punished." He looked at Nate. "My thanks, Alpha, for not condemning the children."

"Did you really expect me to?"

"No, not really. I've known you for too long to believe that of you, but . . . I wasn't sure how much the past few days might have changed you."

Nate nodded. "I can understand that. Now, what do we need to prepare for the Council, and how do we get it to them?"

Jonathan looked thoughtful. "We will need a recording

of all that happened. Each wolf will record an account. We will make a copy of the map showing where the canisters were located and send that, too. Maybe some photos of my scars." Jonathan stopped and glanced from Nate to Garrett. "It would help if you would make a recording of your part in the events, too."

Garrett leaned forward, hands dangling between his wide-spread knees. "I will do so."

Nate watched the expressions fleeting across Garrett's face. "You have something you want to say?"

"I do." He looked down at the floor for several breaths and seemed unable to meet Nate's gaze. "The Queen's name is Lorena. She probably already has statements prepared to send to the Council that the pack threatened her. If I know her, and I think I do, she will try to convince them that the attack was retaliation for some breach of honor by your pack or the previous Alpha."

"You know her that well?"

Garrett's head bobbed. "She's my sister." Garrett still stared at the floor and didn't see Nate frown. Jonathan growled. "She killed my mate to become Queen of the clowder. I was given the choice to support her or leave. I left."

Nate turned an open palm toward Jonathan. The growls stopped, but the heightened tension in the room was still palpable. "Garrett." When Garrett didn't look up, Nate growled. "Garrett."

Garrett raised an expressionless face to him, but Nate could see the anguish in his eyes. "Yes, Alpha?"

"You've been accepted into my pack, Garrett. You

have nothing to fear here." Nate's thumb tapped the desk, but when Garrett and Jonathan both watched his thumb, Nate stopped. *I need to remember not to do that.* "You must know that if your sister is behind this attack, she'll be punished accordingly."

"I know. And she should be." Garrett swallowed. "Nate . . . Alpha, I have been clanless and homeless, by *were* standards, since I left the clowder. You've accepted me into the pack. I will not betray you."

Nate heard the sincerity in Garrett's voice. He gave Garrett a tight smile. "That's all I need to know." He glanced at Jonathan, saw the other man hesitate, then nod. "That's all either of us needed to know."

From downstairs, a loud bell clanged. Nate glanced at the office door, then raised an eyebrow toward Jonathan.

"That's the dinner bell." Jonathan clapped his hands together. "What say we worry about all this after getting some grub?"

Nate grinned. "Grub sounds good about now. You hungry, Garrett?" He grinned again. "Guess I should call you Ben, now."

Garrett nodded. "I suppose you should. And I'm starved."

"Then let's go."

Chapter 18

Early the next morning, Nate leaned against the office window jamb and sipped coffee while staring out the window. For as far as he could see, massive live oak trees filled the landscape. Closer in, a crop sprouted in a furrowed field, a dappling of green showing in rows. Several buildings and houses circled the yard. Beyond the barn and the warehouse was a stock tank Jonathan told him was filled with catfish. In the yard below his window, in the shadow of a gazebo raised on stilts above a picnic table, Reese and Bobby were tossing a baseball. Several of the girls were gathered around the picnic table below the gazebo floor, watching them.

Movement caught his attention. Janelle and two of the girls, Lisa and Amelie, he thought, were walking from the warehouse to the house. Janelle carried a basket with a cloth cover over the contents. He turned at a tap on the office door. Jonathan stood outside the open door, waiting to be invited in.

Nate raised an eyebrow and motioned him to come in. "You don't have to knock, you know."

"Before, uh, everything, no one was allowed to enter the office without permission."

"Well, this is after. I'm not that formal. Have a seat and tell me what's on your mind."

Jonathan sat, back straight.

"You always sit so stiffly?"

"What? Oh, no." Jonathan shifted uncomfortably. "I

just don't know what the rules are, yet."

"The rules." Nate sat in the high-backed executive chair. "Hmm. Neither do I. Guess that makes us about even on that score." He grinned at Jonathan. "Relax. I'm going to need a second in command, and an advisor or two. If you're up to it, I would like you to be my second. Both you and Garrett will be my advisors."

Jonathan let out a slow breath. He leaned forward, hands on his knees. "You trust the cat?"

"Don't have a reason not to. I've known him for nearly 15 years. We didn't always get along, but I think that's because subconsciously I knew there was something different about him." Nate took another sip of coffee. "He's never done anything that would remove my trust."

Jonathan's gaze searched Nate's face. After a moment, he slowly nodded. "Okay."

Nate picked up a folder. "I've been looking over some of the investments. Do you know what's in this file?"

"Records of stocks and bonds."

"Do you know what these are worth?"

"Enough that we don't have to worry about money in this lifetime."

"Huh. This ranch and its owners are billionaires."

Jonathan laughed. "When you have generations of Alphas working to create wealth, it happens."

"The papers all have Randal Hynson's name as the owner. Who is that?"

"The previous Alpha, Janelle's brother."

"So, she inherits everything?"

"No, as the alpha and Janelle's mate, you inherit everything."

Nate shoved his chair back and started pacing. "Female wolves can't own property?"

"Not unless the Alpha allows it. Randal didn't." Jonathan's gaze followed him back and forth across the room. "Randal was very definitely old school. I suppose it's up to you, now."

Nate came to a stop in front of the window, gazed out for several minutes, and then turned to face Jonathan. "Just how much around here is up to me?"

"Almost everything. You can even decide the menu if you want to."

"And if I don't want to?"

"Nate, you are Alpha. In human terms, you are king. Almighty, almost. The only way anyone here can stop you is to challenge you to death battle. No one here is strong enough to do that. Or would want to, for that matter."

Nate sat at the desk, put his crossed arms on the desktop and leaned forward. Staring at the highly-polished wood surface, lips pursed, he considered his options. It seemed he had none, and yet at the same time, all options were his to decide. He sighed. "How can I take care of all this and work, too?" He raised his face and gazed at Jonathan.

"You don't need to work unless you want to." Jonathan shrugged. "Basically, you're rich. Everything here is yours to command and decide." He leaned back and winced.

"Scars still bothering you?

"Yeah. According to your cat friend, they will probably always pull when I move."

"His name is Ben." Nate didn't realize how sharp his tone was until Jonathan's gaze snapped to his face. He sighed. "Sorry. This all has me a bit on edge."

Expression cautious, Jonathan gave him a single nod. "No problem."

"I know, or at least I think I know, that wolves and panthers are seldom friendly, but Ben is part of this pack. I don't want him to feel unwelcome or unwanted."

Another single nod. "As you wish."

Nate muttered a curse and stood up. Both hands pressed flat against the desktop, he leaned toward Jonathan. "Stop that!"

Jonathan blinked several times, his mouth open. "S . . . sir?" he finally got out.

"I may be Alpha, through no fault or desire of my own, but I don't want a toady bowing and scraping to me. I need you to man up, wolf up, I don't know, whatever you have to 'up' to be a partner. If I don't like your suggestions, I'll tell you so, but contrary to what you seem to think, I won't knock your head off for making them."

After several tense moments, Jonathan cleared his throat. "You're serious, aren't you?"

"I am."

The two men stared at each other. After a bit, Jonathan grinned. "You need to be patient, Alpha. You will take some getting used to."

"Yeah. I suppose it's nearly as hard for you as it is for me." Nate sighed and met Jonathan's grin with one of his own. "For now, more than anything, I need a teacher. That's your job, Jonathan. Teach me what I need to know to keep the pack safe."

"If you really want to know," Jonathan waited for Nate's impatient nod. "The first thing you need to do is claim Janelle. Until you do, your Alpha status is not secure."

Nate collapsed into his chair. Running both hands, fingers splayed through his hair, he shook his head and sighed. "I don't know how." He held his hands up and stared at his palms. Convulsively, he clenched his fists and then raised his gaze to Jonathan. "Teach me what I need to know."

An hour later, Nate shook his head. "You've got to be kidding."

"I'm afraid not, Nate. Among *were*, the ceremony is more binding than a marriage ceremony between humans. The bond is a pledge to be mates for life. It's a bond you won't be able to break."

Mine! Koreth's annoyed growl rumbled through Nate's mind. Nate blew out a breath through puffed cheeks. "And she has no choice?"

"Once she is claimed, she is mate to the wolf who claims her." For a moment, Jonathan looked uncertain. "Nate, it is the way of the pack. Janelle knows this, and never expected anything else. The fact that you've put it off so long confuses her. It even hurts her, because she thinks you don't want her when Koreth so obviously wants Nadrai."

"So, when should it be done?"

"Tomorrow, tonight, now. Whenever you decide to do it."

Nate swiveled his chair and stared at the clouds moving slowly above the ranch trees. He thought about

Janelle's reaction the previous day when she thought he didn't want her. Her embarrassment and shame stung him. *Might as well get it over with*, he thought, and mentally laughed at Koreth's eager frolicking. *Take it easy.* He swiveled to face Jonathan. "Let's get it done, then, before the cats come back."

Chapter 19

Nate walked into the kitchen, Jonathan close on his heels. "Janelle, use the bell and call everyone. Send everyone to the gazebo for a meeting."

Without waiting for her to comply, he walked out the door. The bell clanged, calling the wolves to the kitchen. A few moments later, they all followed Janelle to the gazebo. Ben came from the barn, wiping his hands on an oily rag. After they all gathered, Nate took Janelle's hand and led her up the gazebo stairs. He could feel Koreth's pent-up energy bouncing through him. At the top of the stairs, he walked into the center of the gazebo and turned to face Janelle.

"I think it's about time to make things official." When her eyes grew wide, he grinned. "Janelle, by pack law, I claim you as my mate."

She drew a quick breath and released it just as fast. Before she could speak, Nate pulled her into an embrace and kissed her. His hand wound into her hair, holding her head still while he claimed her mouth. She whimpered and leaned into him. When he pulled back, his hand still wrapped in her hair, he studied her for a moment, then he whispered, "Are you sure?"

The trust and sincerity on her face caused him to swallow hard. "I'm sure," she whispered back.

Nate nodded. "I don't know if I can prevent the shift when the medallion comes off."

"Koreth knows what must happen, Nate. He won't

shift until it is time."

He swallowed again. "Remove the medallion for me."

As her hands brought the chain up behind his head, he bowed his head to make it easier for her to remove it. Once it was in her hand, the hand he pressed against her back moved to catch her wrist. He kissed the back of her fingers, then together, they set the medallion on the gazebo rail.

As soon as it left their fingers, Nate felt the urge to shift. Then he felt Koreth take control of the change process and stop it. He took a shaky breath. His arm went back around Janelle, and he pulled her closer. "Jonathan said I would know what to do at this point." He cleared his throat and felt his face redden. "I . . . I really want to bite you."

Janelle's silvery laugh caressed him. "You must. It's part of the mating." She leaned her head to the right, offering her neck to him.

As Nate leaned forward, he felt his mouth shiver, and he realized his face was changing. Unable to stop himself, he clamped his teeth on Janelle's shoulder just below her neck. A thrill shot through him. For a moment, he closed his eyes, able to do nothing but feel the sensation of her blood trickling down his throat and the raw power that surged through his body.

Janelle moaned and pressed against him. He opened his eyes and gently licked her wound. When he could move again, he lifted his head, conscious that his face was once again human. Janelle unbuttoned the top button on his shirt and spread the collar open. Almost immediately, Nate felt her teeth close on his shoulder. The shudder that zinged through him almost knocked him off his feet. He clasped her tighter, as he felt her suck his blood, and heard her swallow. A moment later, he felt her soft tongue lick the wound and felt it begin to heal.

Mine! he heard Koreth growl, then he heard a new voice in his mind. *Yours!*

Startled, he leaned back and looked at Janelle. She tilted her head and smiled. "Nate, meet Nadrai."

Well met, Nate.

Nate blinked, then grinned. "You once said something about hearing each other's wolves after being mated, didn't you?"

"I did. We can also hear each other. Except for rare instances, time and space cannot disrupt our contact." *Hello, Koreth.*

Well met, Janelle.

"Um, Jonathan said . . .."

Janelle laughed. "It is time for our wolves to consummate our union. Our time will be later." She shimmered into the shift.

Koreth took over, forcing the shift. He nipped Nadrai. The two wolves played, rolling around, nipping each other, then Koreth pushed her to the gazebo floor. Embarrassed, Nate could feel Janelle's excited amusement as Koreth took Nadrai as his mate. Below the gazebo, the pack howled their approval, and then quietly left the area to give them some privacy.

*****

Nate opened his eyes, startled to see Nadrai leaning over him. Her tongue slurped over his cheek, and she

102

rested her head on his chest. Careful not to dislodge her, Nate sat up and stroked the soft white fur between her ears. "What's wrong, beautiful?"

Nadrai twitched one of her ears, then shimmered. A moment later, he held Janelle in his arms. "You really think Nadrai is beautiful, Nate?"

"I think you both are beautiful." Several strands of her blonde moonlight hair blew across her face. Nate gently swept them behind her ear. He cleared his throat. "So, we're mated."

"Mated. Married. Joined. Whatever you want to call it."

He nodded. "You're okay with that." His statement had a bit of question in it.

"I am." She took his face in her hands. "Nate, I am not only okay with it, I am happy with it." Her gaze searched his face. "I hope you are."

A slow smile spread across his face. "I am. I just wanted to make sure you were, too."

"You worry too much." Janelle laughed. "I need to go to the house and prepare for our First Night."

"First Night?"

"Jonathan didn't tell you?"

"Tell me what?" He felt his eyes grow wide. "We don't have to do, uh, that, in front of them, do we?"

Janelle laughed. "No. The public portion of our union is over. The rest is private, just between the two of us." She gently touched his lip. "You are a Royal Alpha. Unless we want pups right away, I have to take precautions."

"Pups? Babies?"

"Um. At least two at a time."

103

Nate swallowed. "Two?"

He could imagine the look of terror on his face when she laughed. "I'm just kidding. It happens, but not often. Besides, I'm not in heat, right now."

"In heat." While she pushed herself to her feet, Nate cleared his throat. When he thought he controlled himself, he stood up and looked down at her. "I . . . I think I might like to have . . . pups with you . . . someday."

She tilted her head and studied him. He felt his face redden again. "I never really thought about it," he said. "I wasn't attracted to women before I met you. I believed I would never be, uh, married, or have kids."

"Wolves are seldom attracted to human women. It happens, but rarely." Reaching past him, Janelle retrieved the medallion from the rail. "Don't forget this."

Nate took it from her fingers, and looked at it, then looked at her. "Why didn't I shift when I took it off? And how did I change back without it?"

"Koreth controlled the shift. My suspicion is that you will no longer need it to stay human. You may even be able to shift while wearing it. Most adult Royals can."

Nate slipped it over his head. *Okay, Koreth. Let's see if we can shift while wearing this.* Several seconds passed before Nate felt the familiar tingle that started the shimmer into a wolf. Koreth barked, and jumped up on Janelle, licking her face.

Janelle laughed and gave him a tight hug. "I love you, too, Koreth!"

Suddenly, still in her embrace, he shimmered into Nate. "You love Koreth?"

For a moment, she was very still, then she smiled. Her smile warmed all the dark places in Nate's soul. "Yes. I love Koreth. I love you, too, Nate." With that, she pressed her lips against his.

Nate pulled her tight and returned the kiss with as much fervor as she gave. When he pulled back, he nuzzled her ear. "What's this about First Night?"

"You'll have to wait until tonight to find out." Laughing, she whirled out of his arms and skipped down the gazebo steps. With flying feet, she ran to the house, slamming the door behind her as she entered the kitchen.

Chapter 20

Bemused, Nate watched her precipitous flight. After the door slammed behind her, he shook his head and grinned. "Tonight? Sounds like this will be interesting, to say the least." He heard someone clear their throat and looked over the rail to see Garrett walk to the table beneath the gazebo and sit.

"No rest for the weary," he muttered, and quickly descended the steps. He walked to the table and sat opposite Garrett. "Everything okay, Ben?"

"Hmm? Oh, yes." Garrett studied Nate, then grinned. "Everything okay with you?"

When Nate blushed, Garrett laughed. "Sorry. Couldn't help it." He leaned forward. "I'd like to discuss a few things if you have time."

Nate nodded. "What things?"

"I've been on the force for nearly thirty-five years. I've wanted to retire for a while, but there was nothing else for me to do." Garrett stopped for a moment, then said in a rush, "Nate, someone needs to train your young wolves to fight. Their wolves can fight, I have no doubt, but they need some hand-to-hand training, too. If you don't mind, I'd like to be that someone." He shrugged. "I know you could do it, but as Alpha, your days will often be filled with other matters." He stopped and watched Nate.

Nate could tell Garrett was trying to gauge his reaction to the suggestion. *It's a good idea,* said Koreth.

Nate turned his attention to Koreth. *You think it would help to have the kids learn combat skills?*

They must learn to fight. Jonathan can teach the wolves, but the cat . . . At Nate's annoyed snort, Koreth stopped, then continued. *They need Ben to teach them combat skills.*

Amused that Koreth corrected himself, Nate decided to think of Garrett as Ben from that moment. Nate nodded. *I think you are right.*

Ben was beginning to look a bit concerned when Nate returned his attention to him. "If it's not a good . . .."

"It's a great idea. I don't know why I didn't think of it, myself. Koreth agrees. You have the job." Nate held his hand out to Ben and Ben shook it, an eyebrow raised.

"You don't act much like a wolf."

"Didn't know I was a wolf until a couple of days ago." He lifted the medallion and held it up. "This kept me from being able to shift, and it keeps other *were* from sensing me as a wolf."

Ben nodded. "I knew there was something different about you. You just didn't smell right to be human, but it never occurred to me that you were *were*."

"So, it was as much a surprise to you as it was to me."

Ben laughed and shook his head. "I sincerely doubt that." He scratched his balding head. "Nate, it won't take all my time to teach the kids. If you don't mind, I'd also like to mechanic a bit." He grinned a bit sheepishly. "Always did love getting grease under my fingernails. Not many cats do, but there's just something about it."

"I'm sure there are plenty of vehicles here that will need a mechanic at some point. Why don't you see if any of the kids are interested and teach one or two of them those skills, as well." Nate turned to look around the ranch. "Your most important position will be as an advisor to me."

When he heard Ben choke, he spun around and looked at him. "I'm serious, Ben. This *were* world is all new to me. Jonathan will do what he can to get me up to speed on wolf matters, but I need someone who can look beyond just wolf and help me when other things come up. I'll need someone I can count on when we deal with the Council."

Ben sat very still for a moment, then nodded. "I'm honored to be an advisor to the Alpha."

"When you go back to turn in your resignation, will you take mine with you?"

"You're going to take the manager position for the ranch?"

"I am. I'll probably make a mess of it, but for now, at least, I think my place is here on the ranch."

Ben smiled. "I'll take both our resignations in tomorrow morning. I'll need your service pistol and badge, so I can turn them in. We both have several weeks of vacation built up. I'll put us on vacation for the last weeks of employment." He laughed. "No point in losing it. Oh, after lunch, I thought I might take a quick trip to the cave and get the rest of your gear for you."

"Sounds good. Take Jonathan or one of the boys with you, in case you have trouble." Nate stood up. "I'll have to review the books before I give you a salary offer."

"No problem. A place to stay and food to eat is enough for now. We can discuss anything else later."

The dinner bell rang. After a quick glance at the house, Nate sniffed the air and grinned at Ben. "Smells like steak. Let's go eat."

*****

While most of the teens watched television or helped Janelle clean up the kitchen, Reese and Bobby patrolled outside the house. Nate, Jonathan, and Ben retired to the office. Nate rolled his chair to the wall left of his desk and opened a cabinet. He pointed to a safe nestled inside. "I need to find out what's in this. Do you know the combination, Jonathan?"

Jonathan shook his head. "Randal never told anyone, unless it was Janelle."

Janelle, please come to the office for a minute.

Be right there.

Nate pulled a sheaf of papers off the shelf above the safe. "I found the birth and death records for the past century." He handed them to Jonathan. "Since I don't know the names of all the deceased, I need you to take care of this."

Jonathan nodded. "I'll complete it and bring it back to you tomorrow afternoon. Do you want me to have the first watch again tonight?"

"Yes. We'll keep the same schedule for a few days so that we can all have some consistency to our days."

Janelle stepped into the office. "You asked to see me, Nate?"

109

"Do you know the safe combination?"

"Oh." She bit her lip, then shook her head. "No, but I know where Randal kept it. I was forbidden to use it while he lived, but he wanted someone to be able to open it, just in case . . .." She swallowed and blinked back tears. "I'll get it."

Nate listened to her steps rush down the hall, then a door opened. He looked at Jonathan, then at Ben. "While we wait, Ben, I need to know if you think the cats will use poison again."

Ben frowned and considered the idea for a minute before shaking his head. "I don't believe so. Even if they realize there are still wolves alive, they will believe there are so few they have the power to overthrow you."

Nate felt Koreth tense. The tension radiated into his own neck and shoulders. He rolled his neck to ease his muscles. "Do they?"

"No. You may not fully understand your Alpha abilities, yet, but Koreth knows them. The only way they could beat you at this point is if they could surprise you." He glanced at Jonathan and looked back at Nate. "There's no way that will happen."

Janelle walked into the office. A flat turquoise stone dangled from a chain in her hand. She handed the pendant to Nate. "The combination is etched on the back."

Nate shook his head. "That's different." He turned the pendant over and used the numbers etched into the back to unlock the safe, then turned the handle and opened it. Inside were three stacks of cash about three

110

inches high on the top shelf. On the bottom shelf, there was a small leather pouch. Nate picked up one stack of cash and used his thumb to fan through the bills in succession. All were one-hundred-dollar bills. With a guttural huff, he set the bills back in the safe and picked up the leather pouch. Beneath it, he found a single page folded into quarters.

He glanced at Janelle, and she shrugged. "I've never seen inside the safe."

He picked up the folded paper and opened it. After reading it, he took a sharp breath, folded the paper and slipped it into his pocket. As he did, his hand brushed the silver tip he removed from the cat. Nate frowned and took it from his pocket. Janelle and Jonathan both gasped. When Nate looked up, they stared at the silver in his hands in disbelief. Right eyebrow raised, Nate looked at each in turn, then looked at Janelle.

"What's wrong?"

"You can touch silver without burning." Janelle sounded as if she were almost strangling.

He nodded. "I think it has something to do with the medallion. It isn't comfortable, but it doesn't hurt."

Janelle and Jonathan exchanged wide-eyed glances.

Nate tapped his knee with his thumb for a moment, then cleared his throat. "Okay. I'll bite. Why are you so upset?"

"It's just that . . .," Janelle looked at Jonathan again.

"Only a pureblood Royal can handle silver, Nate," said Jonathan. "Even with the medallion, you should at least blister a bit."

"So?"

"According to our documents, the last pureblood royal

of record died more than 20 years ago. He was found on a rural farm in Nebraska. Someone ripped his throat open and clawed his heart."

Nate frowned. "When exactly did that happen?"

"Twenty-two years ago, last January."

Nate felt a shiver traverse his spine. Twenty-two years ago. "Royals kill each other?"

"There was a rumor that the lost pack was located. The Colorado Royal went to check it out. When he didn't return, his pack found him in the backyard of a farmhouse. Another man was dead in the house. He was *were*, but there was no reason anyone would think he was a Royal. There was no one else there."

"If he was royal, why would royals kill each other?"

Ben sighed. "For the same reason, my sister killed my wife, Nate. Greed for power."

Nate walked to the window and stared out into the darkness. Twenty-two years. For twenty-two years, he had nightmares about a werewolf stalking him. For twenty-two years, he had told himself over and over that his dad was not a werewolf, that he did not see him shift as he died. In his mind, he heard Koreth whine and ignored him.

When he spoke, Nate's tone was so flat and emotionless he didn't recognize his own voice. "How could killing another Royal give him more power?"

"I don't know," said Jonathan and Ben at the same time.

Janelle didn't answer. Nate turned to look at her. Her eyes were filled with sorrow for the pain she could feel embracing him. He quirked an eyebrow at her. "Do you know?"

She nodded. "The medallion." She cleared her throat. "One gives you the ability to hide your *were* abilities and identity. I was told that having more than one enhances your abilities. For a Royal, that would make him almost invincible."

Nate took a deep breath. Without a word, he handed her the leather pouch. At her questioning look, he nodded toward the pouch. "Open it."

Janelle carefully untied the leather thongs holding the pouch closed, then gently shook a medallion into her hand. It was an identical match to the one Nate wore.

Chapter 21

For several long minutes, no one spoke, then the three facing Nate began speaking at once.

"It matches your medallion," said Janelle.

"There are two of them?" asked Jonathan.

"What happens if you wear both?" asked Ben.

Nate held up his hand. "Yes, there are two of them, and they look the same. If I own everything on the ranch, I suppose that means I have two of them." He looked at each, in turn, waiting for their nods. "I don't know what happens. Maybe we should find out."

He took the second medallion from Janelle. After studying it for a moment, he slipped it over his head, then pulled the one his father gave him out and held them side by side. He shrugged. "It doesn't seem to do anything." As he finished speaking, the second medallion jerked out of his fingers and melded to the first with a brilliant, lightning blue flash. He dropped the pendant and shook his hand. "Ouch!"

Janelle caught her breath. "Nate, look."

Nate glanced down at his chest. The medallion glowed a blue so pale it was white at the edges. The glow grew brighter, then shot pencil-thin beams of light into Nate's eyes. "Ahhh!" Nate fell to his knees, unable to close his eyes as the light continued to shine.

Vaguely, he heard Janelle's startled scream, and Jonathan shout, "Nate!"

Koreth howled, first in pain, then the howls changed to excited barks. The wolf stretched, growing in Nate's mind, then suddenly a wolf manifested on the floor before Nate. The light flashed once, then died. Nate blinked and gasped for breath, just then realizing that he was not breathing while the light bathed his face.

Koreth whined and leaned against Nate, his sandpaper tongue licking Nate's face. "What happened?"

We are one, and we are two. Koreth tilted his head to the side and studied Nate.

"We're separate?"

Only for a time. We will become one, again.

"I don't understand," Nate whispered.

This is the power of twin medallions. From this point, we will be one when you are awake unless you will us to be two. When you are sleeping, we will be two. I will guard the pack while you rest.

Nate blinked, then looked up at Janelle. Janelle's gaze was locked on Koreth. Face pale, she swallowed and shook her head as if she couldn't believe what she was seeing. "Are . . . are you okay, Nate?"

"I think so." Nate stood, swaying a bit until his head cleared. "Koreth says we don't need a guard at night. He will guard the pack."

We can also call forth others to guard. Koreth watched him, tongue hanging out of his mouth. *Call forth Nadrai so we can play.*

Nate glanced at Janelle. "Did you hear that?"

"I did." She swallowed again. "How does it work? Does it hurt?"

It is like the first shift. After that, it will not hurt.

"Koreth says it only hurts the first time."

She nodded. "I heard."

"Nate, can you do this for everyone?" asked Jonathan. "If you can, we could all get rested up without worrying about an attack. The wolves could protect us until we were

115

up and ready."

The Alpha can so command. Nate nodded. "Koreth says I can command the wolves to separate."

Ben sank into one of the office chairs. "Do you know what this means?" At Nate's raised eyebrow, he leaned forward. "It means that our effective fighting force just doubled."

Jonathan bit his lip thoughtfully and nodded. "We could ask the wolves to set up a solid perimeter around the ranch."

Janelle shook her head. "I don't think so. Some of the kids are getting close to mating age. Their wolves shouldn't run loose without supervision."

I will not allow mating while there is danger! At Koreth's indignant tone, Nate and Janelle grinned at each other.

"Looks like that worry is taken care of." Nate looked down at the conjoined medallion. *What would happen if I wore three of these?*

From the beginning, wearing more than two was forbidden.

Nate frowned. *Why?*

Power is seductive. Too much power destroys. Koreth whined. *It is my onus to protect you from destruction. I cannot allow more medallions.* Koreth stood on his hind legs and licked Nate's jaw. *The power you have now is hidden even from you. Only should you need it, will it appear.*

"For my own good."

For our good. Koreth dropped to four feet and pranced. *Bring forth Nadrai. We will watch while you sleep.*

Nate sighed. "I don't know how," he said aloud.

116

Hold the medallion, touch Janelle, and command that she be two.

Nate picked up Janelle's hand. "I won't do this unless you agree."

He could see the fear that filled her eyes, but she slowly nodded. "If Koreth thinks it should be, do it."

After a glance at Jonathan and Ben, he nodded. "Okay." He pressed his palm gently against her face. "I command you to be two."

Janelle cried out in pain and fell against Nate. "I'm sorry," he whispered into her hair. The air shimmered behind her, then Nadrai manifested next to Koreth. As Janelle sagged in Nate's arms, Nadrai yipped happily and started running. Koreth followed her, his bark playful. Both ran out of the open office door and down the stairs.

Moments later, they heard shouts and glass break as the two wolves burst into the living room. Janelle looked up at Nate and giggled. "I think we better get them outside where they can play without breaking anything."

Nate laughed. "I think you're right."

Hand in hand, they rushed down the stairs. Koreth chased Nadrai around the sofa set in the center of the room, while teens stood on the furniture watching, mouths open. Janelle opened the front door and called Nadrai. Spying the chance to enhance the chase, Nadrai barked and ran outside, Koreth right behind her. Janelle let the spring pull the screen door shut, then turned and grinned at Nate. "They'll be back after getting rid of some of their energy."

Together they turned to face the teens. Jonathan and Ben stood at the bottom of the stairs watching them, too. Nate blew his breath out puffed cheeks, then grinned. "My guess is that you're all a bit confused."

The teens all glanced at each other, then nodded. Behind Nate, the screen door opened. Reese and Bobby rushed in. "Hey, what are Koreth and Nadr . . .." Reese's words tumbled to a stop when he saw Nate and Janelle standing in front of him. "How . . .?"

Nate motioned for everyone to sit down. "Everyone knows about my medallion, right?" He looked at each in turn. "Well, there was another like it in the safe. When I put it on, it gave me the ability to split into wolf and man at the same time. It gave me the power to split pack wolves into wolf and human."

Alarm showed on the faces of several teens. "It's only temporary," he assured them. "Koreth suggests that we split the pack at night so that the wolves can guard while we sleep. I think it's a good idea," he held his hand up to stop the mutters, "but I won't force anyone. I'll try to answer your questions, but just understand that all this is new to me."

Lisa took her index finger away from her mouth. She'd chewed the nail almost into the quick. "Um, what if we get stuck that way?"

Janelle walked to the girl and gave her a tight hug. "Nate and Koreth won't let that happen."

Lisa glanced at Nate.

"That's right. Koreth and I will make sure you return to be together."

Bobby grinned at Lisa. "Our wolves could play." He twitched an eyebrow at her.

Nate cleared his throat. "None of that. Until allowed by either Koreth or myself, there will be no dating or mating." Though he was never inclined to date the girls he knew in his teens, he remembered how the other boys acted. He drew his eyes down into a severe frown.

118

"Is that understood?"

One by one, the teens nodded. Several of the boys swallowed nervously, while most of the girls looked relieved. "Okay. I don't fully understand how this works. I might be able to do this for all of you at once, but without Koreth, I don't want to try. I will do this one at a time."

"Will it hurt?" asked Amelie.

"A bit." Janelle's soft smile seemed to take the sting out of her words. "But, it won't be any worse than the first change. And it will let us all get some badly needed rest tonight."

Reese was the first to step forward. "I'll go first."

Nate noticed the surprise that flashed across Janelle's and Jonathan's faces and wondered about it. He nodded and motioned for Reese to step closer. Hand on the boy's shoulder, he said, "I command you to become two."

After all the wolves left the house to join Koreth and Nadrai, Nate looked at Ben. "I don't know if it works on cats, too."

"That's okay. At my age, I don't think I want that kind of new adventure, anyway." Ben shuddered.

Nate laughed and clapped a hand on his shoulder. "You're not that old, old man."

"Old enough to know better than to mess with wolf magic."

Sobered, Nate nodded.

Chapter 22

Without the restless energy from their wolves, the teens soon tired and were ready to retire for the evening. Jonathan sent them to their preselected rooms, then yawned. "Think I'll go to bed, too."

Ben grinned. "Me, too. Old bones need more sleep."

Nate covered Janelle's hand with his. "You keep saying you're old, Ben, but you couldn't be as old as you keep hinting."

Ben's eyes crinkled. Merriment danced across his expression. "How old do you think I am, Nate?"

"I dunno." Nate shrugged. "Forty, fifty at the most. Wait, you said you've been on the force for thirty-five years."

At that, Ben burst out laughing. "I was fifty many decades before you were born. *Were* don't age the way humans do, so once they reach maturity, it is difficult to judge ages." When Nate blinked at him, he laughed again. "I'm a hundred and seventy-five. That's one reason I decided to quit my job. I've been in one place too long, and people will start to notice, soon."

Eyes wide, Nate looked at Janelle and Jonathan. Janelle caught his hand within both of hers. "Nate, I'm twenty-four, but before everything happened, I was barely considered more than a pup." She jerked her head toward Jonathan. "Jonathan is eighty-three, next month."

"You're kidding, right?" Nate looked at each of the

other three adults in turn and sighed when they all shook their heads. "Guess I still have a lot to learn."

Janelle laughed and squeezed his hand. "You can learn it later." She leaned closer to him and whispered, "It's our First Night."

Nate turned his head to meet her gaze. "First Night." He leaned forward until his mouth was next to her ear. "So, what does that mean?"

"It means . . .," still holding his hand, she turned to the other men. "Goodnight, guys. See you in the morning."

With Jonathan's and Ben's snickers behind him, Nate let her pull him toward the stairs.

*****

Nate slowly awakened to the warmth of Janelle's body pressed against his. Her head was on his shoulder, his arm snuggling her close. Without opening his eyes, he reveled in the feel of her, reliving the night before. A smile tugged at the corners of his lips. She smelled like summer jasmine. He turned to press a kiss on the top of her head. Janelle murmured in her sleep, and he thought about waking her up to see if she was interested in a first morning. Just as he decided to wake her, the foot of the bed dipped sharply, and two heavy bodies landed on top of them.

His eyes popped open just as a face full of Koreth shoved at him and a tongue lapped him from chin to forehead. Next to him, Janelle was similarly treated by Nadrai, then the two wolves barked and yipped while bouncing around to change places and wolf-kissed their human's mates. Janelle started laughing, wrestling with Koreth, while Nate put his arms around Nadrai and hugged her.

Chuckling, he glanced at Janelle. "Looks like it's time to get up."

"Looks like." She pushed Koreth off her. "Move, big guy. I can't get up with you on top of me." Koreth barked and pushed her back down, his long tongue slurping her face, again. Giggling so hard she could barely breathe, she pushed him without much effect.

"Whoa, Koreth," said Nate. "You have to let her breathe." Before he finished speaking, Koreth yipped and turned his ministrations to Nate. *It's time to get up. The wolves want to go home.*

"Okay, Koreth. I'm up. I'm up." Nate lightly pushed Koreth to the side and rolled out of bed onto his feet. "See, I'm up."

"So much for first-morning fun," he said, grinning and shrugging at Janelle.

She laughed and tossed his t-shirt at him. "Werewolves have long lives, Nate. You will have many mornings to play."

*****

Coffee cup in hand, Nate pulled out a swiveling stool at the kitchen bar, sat, and watched while Janelle fried bacon. "You sure you don't want help?"

Janelle laughed and shook her head. "I've been doing this for years. Cooking is one of my favorite things to do."

Nate grinned and took a sip of his coffee. "That's great. Eating is one of my favorite things to do, so we should get along just fine."

She snickered and tossed a pot holder at him. Nate snagged it out of the air and tossed it back. She caught it and turned back to frying bacon.

Nate took another sip. "The kids were really glad to be reunited with their wolves."

Without turning, she nodded. "Um. I think their wolves were happy, too."

Footsteps shuffled down the hall toward the kitchen. Nate swiveled his stool and nodded at Ben. "Morning."

Ben nodded in return and stopped at the coffee pot. A moment later, cup in hand, he took a cautious sip, then blew on his coffee. "Morning. Coffee's a bit hot."

"Better than cold." Nate waved at one of the three vacant stools. "Have a sit."

"Thanks." Ben settled onto the stool and sighed while rolling his neck.

Nate raised an eyebrow. "Sleep okay?"

"Yeah. Just have a kink in my neck this morning. It was nice to get a full night's rest." He grinned at Janelle's smile. "Breakfast smells fantastic."

"It'll be done in a bit. The bacon is done, biscuits are almost ready, and the eggs won't take long." Janelle used tongs to lift the last several strips of bacon from the pan. She lifted a paper towel and arranged them atop the pile of cooked bacon on the platter, then recovered them.

Nate set his cup on the bar. "You still plan to go to work today?"

"I'm scheduled today, so I'll be going in. You still want

me to turn in your resignation?"

Janelle dropped her tongs and turned to face Nate. "You're resigning your job?"

"I think I will be too busy sorting things out here at the ranch to be gone ten hours a day, don't you?" Nate watched her closely. It hadn't occurred to him that he needed to discuss his decision with her. "Is there a problem?" He studied the expressions fleeting across her face. Concern, relief, and then happiness.

She smiled and shook her head. "I just didn't know if you would want to quit your job." Her face colored with a flush of pink, and she turned back to her cooking. "I feel better having you here, just in case the . . .."

Her words faltered. She turned off the stove burner and bowed her head. Her pain hit Nate in waves. He slid off the stool, stepped around the bar, and cradled her back against his chest. For a moment, she was very still, then she whipped around in his arms and buried her face in his chest. Sobs tore through her. "I just can't forget the . . . the children. What they did to them . . . what I saw."

Nate heard Ben slide off the stool behind him and peered over his shoulder. Ben raised a hand and nodded, then quietly left the kitchen. Turning his attention back to Janelle, Nate quietly stroked her back with his left hand.

He pressed his cheek against the top of her head. "It's over, Janelle. I won't let it happen again."

He continued holding her and stroking her back until her sobs eased. When she stopped crying, she took several deep, gasping breaths, before relaxing against him. Her hands clutched at his shirt and she pressed her face deeper into his shoulder. Nate caressed her hair, then gently turned her face up to his. His lips brushed against her forehead. "I'm not going anywhere, Janelle. I promise."

She blinked and studied his face. He knew she could feel the sincerity of his promise. With a smile, he gently kissed her lips. He was surprised when her arms wound around his neck and she raised up on her toes to return the kiss. His tongue gently pushed against her lips, until she surrendered her mouth to him. He pulled her body tighter against him.

"Eewww!" exclaimed several voices.

Nate broke the kiss and looked at the door. All the teens were peeking around the door frame. Janelle sniffed, let out a breath, and then laughed. She pulled Nate's face around, gave him another quick kiss, then stepped back. "I better get the eggs done, or the biscuits will burn."

Fingers trailing along her arm as she turned away, Nate let her go back to cooking. Eyebrows raised, he turned back to the kids. "Someone set the table."

Boys snickered and girls giggled while they rushed to obey. Soon everyone sat around the huge farm-style dining table. Trying to keep his surveillance unobtrusive, Nate watched them chat while they ate. He hadn't been around teens much since he left his foster-parent's home and still didn't know some of their names. It was . . . interesting to watch them interact.

He felt Janelle's hand touch his knee and quirked an eyebrow at her. She smiled and he choked on his biscuit. He hadn't seen such trust in another's eyes since he saw

125

his mom look at his dad the night before his dad was killed.

For a moment, he was overwhelmed with the responsibility her trust entailed. *We are Alpha.* Koreth sniffed, and Nate grinned at his wolf's disdain. *She is our mate. She trusts us. We will protect her. We will protect and nurture the pack.* Nate nodded.

At Janelle's questioning look, Nate grinned. "You didn't hear Koreth?"

Janelle shook her head. "I only hear him when he wants me to."

"Didn't know that." He covered the hand on his knee with his own. "Koreth and I will protect you." He swept his gaze over a suddenly quiet group. "All of you."

Chapter 23

After two hours of steady driving, Ben pulled into his designated parking spot. He picked up the satchel that contained Nate's Glock and both their resignations from the seat beside him. As he walked to the PD door, a uniformed officer waved and held the door open for him.

"Morning, Captain."

"Good morning, Jenkins." Ben nodded and stepped inside. The smell of werepanther brought him up short. At Jenkins' questioning look, Ben reached in his pocket. "Think I'll get a soda before going to the office," he muttered.

Jenkins grinned and continued down the hall. Ben walked to the soda machine, sniffing to see if he could locate the cat. When he identified her, he fumbled, nearly dropping his handful of quarters. *Lorena! What's my sister doing here?* Trying to locate her by scent alone, he dropped coins into the machine and bent to get his soda selection. When he turned, Nate's partner, Eli Thomas, stepped past him to put in his own quarters.

"Good morning, Captain. Have you seen Nate, today?"

"Morning, Thomas. Nate won't be in today." Ben's gaze swept the area. "He's extended his vacation."

Eli Thomas grinned. "Don't blame him." He retrieved his drink, turned to go to his desk, then stopped and looked back. "Oh, you have a visitor. She's waiting in your office."

"Tall brunette? Too much lipstick?"

Thomas laughed. "That's her."

Ben nodded absently. "Thanks. I forgot something in the car. If she asks, tell her I'll be there soon."

"Sure thing."

Ben watched him turn and walk out of the reception area. He swallowed and glanced around. The room was full of people, some being processed for crimes, others reporting crimes. When he couldn't sense any other cats, he popped the top of his soda, took a sip and walked out the door. Without hurry, he walked to his car, opened the door, tossed the satchel back into the passenger's seat, and sat behind the wheel.

After setting his soda can in the cup holder with shaking hands, he pulled his keys from his pocket and started the car. He didn't breathe easy until he pulled onto I 10 headed for the ranch. When safely out of the city, he pulled over onto the shoulder.

He quickly scanned the countryside around him, then pulled his phone from his pocket. After a quick call to let Jenkins know he suddenly wasn't feeling well and had gone home, he called Nate.

When Nate answered, he took a deep breath. "I'm on my way back. The Queen was in the office."

Chapter 24

By the time Ben was back on the ranch, Nate called Jonathan and Janelle into a meeting and worked out some plans. The four youngest wolves, Gayle, Lisa, Owen, and Asher, would stay in the house inside the kitchen. Since the rest would be outside guarding the front and sides of the house, all the four inside needed to do was to keep panthers from coming in the back of the house through the back door.

All the windows and doors were closed and locked, with boards nailed over the windows to slow the cats down if they got that far. Three older teens were stationed at each side of the house, while Nate, Janelle, Jonathan, and Reese were watching the front.

Ben drove into the yard and stopped. Nate watched him lean over for a moment. When he got out, Ben had his pistol in his right hand and Nate's in his left. He quickly walked to Nate, then handed him the gun and holster. "Thought you might need this, so I brought it back."

Nate took the Glock from the holster, chambered a bullet, then slid the gun into the holster and slipped the holster into his waistband. *Best to be prepared.* "Did she see you?"

Ben shook his head. "I don't think so, but someone will tell her I left. I think she will probably come straight here."

"You're sure it was her?"

Eyes narrowed, Ben pressed his lips together and nodded. "I won't ever forget her scent. Not for as long as

I live."

Nate nodded. "You're here with me. Janelle, Reese, and Jonathan will be behind us. If you and I can deal with this, we will. If any of them get past us, the others will do their best."

"Nate, if fighting starts, we'll all be fighting for our lives."

Nate felt his face tighten into a grimace. "Understood." *Koreth, tell the wolves to let the kids know.*

Koreth was eager to join the possible battle. *We should all be two.*

Do I need to call the others here to make us all two?

No. I will command.

Surprised at Koreth's words, Nate looked at Janelle. "Koreth says he can change the others to two without my help once we are two."

"His power grows, as yours does." She nodded. "I think it's a good idea. The wolves won't tire as quickly, and Nadrai tells me she can smell better when we are apart."

Whenever you're ready, Koreth.

Nate felt Koreth gather himself and it seemed he felt the wolf jump right out of his chest. "Ahhh." He staggered for a step, then caught himself.

The air shimmered, and Koreth resolved before him. A shimmering, almost ghostly bronze medallion hung around Koreth's neck. Tongue out, he tilted his massive head and whined. *I gave you pain.*

Only for a minute, my friend. You don't need me to go to the others?

No. Now that they have been through the two-change, they do not need your touch. Koreth stood on his hind legs as he had at the funeral. Slapping his front paws together, he commanded, *Pack, become two.*

With startled cries from their humans, Janelle's, Jonathan's, and Reese's wolves shimmered into existence. From around the corners of the house and from inside, too, Nate heard shouts, then yips of excitement as the pack obeyed Koreth's command. Nate snapped around to face Ben when he heard a wildcat yowl and spit. Ben stood with a stunned expression on his face, looking down at the large, midnight black panther backed up against his feet.

Slowly Ben raised his gaze to Nate and swallowed weakly. "Guess now we know wolf magic works on panther shifters."

"Sorry, Ben. You are part of the pack, and Koreth didn't specify only wolves." Nate squeezed Ben's shoulder. "You okay?"

"Yeah, uh, sure." The pasty color of Ben's face worried Nate. Ben swallowed again. "I mean, I think so. This is disorienting. It's the first time I have ever been separated from Marcel. I think it's harder on him than it is on me."

Nate studied the cat shrinking back against Ben's legs. He dropped to one knee and stretched a hand toward Marcel. "It's okay, Marcel. You are pack. You are safe here."

Marcel watched him through squinted eyes, looked up at Ben, who nodded, then back at Nate. He took an uncertain step forward, tail wrapped tightly around his legs, nose extended to sniff Nate's hand. Nate was still until Marcel tentatively licked his fingers, and gave a soft

131

meow. The tension in Nate's shoulders evaporated. He gently scratched beneath Marcel's jowls and Marcel purred. "We're all family here, Marcel. You are home."

I am honored, Alpha.

Nate smiled. "The honor is mine. You have much you can teach me."

It is customary to refer to an older cat as 'old one.'
Old one, I look forward to learning from you.

For a moment, Nate could have sworn the panther grinned at him. Still smiling, Nate stood up and looked at Ben. Ben regained some of his color and seemed steadier on his feet. "Better?"

"I think so." He gave Nate a weak grin. "Takes some getting used to."

"I'm sure it does. It was strange for me, and I have known Koreth for less than a week."

Marcel snarled. *Cats come!*

Moments later, Nate heard tires crunching gravel as they rushed down the dirt road toward the house. Obviously, Marcel's hearing was better than his own. "Can you tell how many, Marcel?"

Four cars. I cannot tell how many are in them.

Nate glanced at each of the others and gave them a nod. As one, they went to their assigned posts. Nate checked to make sure Janelle was behind him, then turned to face the four cars that screeched to a halt in front of him, spraying gravel. Nate ignored the sting of gravel flying into his legs and took a step forward.

Arms crossed, his expression settled into one his Marine buddies would recognize. The one that told them no one would get past him. The one that told them

132

someone would die if they tried.

Four doors on each car burst open, with at least one person coming out of each, twelve men and four women. Nate felt Koreth brush against his leg but didn't look down at him. A tall brunette wearing too much make-up stepped to the front of the people before him, a younger, black-haired woman behind her.

"That's far enough. You are trespassing. Leave."

The brunette threw her head back and laughed. "I claim this ranch." Then she looked confused. "You are not a wolf. Where is the Alpha?"

Nate and Koreth took a single step forward together. Nate's eyes narrowed. "We are Alpha, cat. This is our ranch." Koreth growled. Nate dropped his hand to the wolf's head, his attention still on the Queen. "Leave. Now!"

Chapter 25

The Queen studied Nate's aggressive stance. Nate raised an eyebrow when her nose wrinkled and she sniffed several times. She looked past Nate and snarled at Ben. "So, this is where you hide, traitor."

The woman behind her gasped. When Nate looked at the younger woman, he was surprised at the shock on her face; shock that quickly gave way to anger.

Nate glanced across at Ben. The man was standing stock still, eyes narrowed, no expression on his face. Marcel, however, was set to pounce. Ben didn't answer.

Is this the woman who killed Ben's mate? thought Nate.

She killed our mate, Marcel told him.

Ben stepped up beside Nate. When he spoke, his voice held no emotion. "I am not the traitor, Lorena. Lauren died by your hand, not mine."

The Queen laughed. "What does it matter? I am your Queen." She pointed at Nate. "Kill him."

"You are not my queen. I will never acknowledge you. Nor will I take your orders."

"Fool! He is wolf and enemy." Spittle flew from her mouth and she stamped her foot.

"Not my enemy. He is my Alpha."

Lorena sneered at him. "You're a coward, just as you've always been, else your wife would not have died."

"She was dead when I returned home. If you hadn't kidnapped my daughter, you would have died then."

"What?" The woman behind the Queen took a step forward. "You didn't kill my mother?"

Nate heard Ben's quick intake of breath. "Flora?"

The young woman nodded. "Aunt Lorena told us all that you killed Mother and ran when the clowder tried to apprehend you." Another step. "Which is true?"

"What does it matter? Your mother died. Your father ran. He was tried and convicted in absentia." Lorena's hands fluttered through the air. "Attack them."

The other cats started forward, but stopped when Flora shouted, "Stop!"

Surprise splashed across her face, the Queen turned to look at the younger woman. "I gave a command."

"And I counter-commanded. I would know the truth of this matter before this goes further."

"You will obey me." Lorena stared at her niece through her cat's eyes.

Flora ignored her. She turned to her father. "Will you allow me to see?"

Ben nodded. "If you must."

When Marcel slinked through the grass to her feet, she raised startled eyes to her father. "How . . .?"

"My Alpha commanded. It is very old, little-known magic."

"Magic." Flora looked at Nate, eyes narrowed. "You have magic, wolf?"

"I do." Expression still set in stone, Nate nodded to Marcel. "Show her what she wants to see, Marcel."

"I will not allow . . .."

135

Nate interrupted the Queen. "You have no choice."

She snarled and took a step toward him. "I will deal with you myself."

Suddenly, the Glock appeared in Nate's hand. "You will be quiet or there will be another cat buried on this ranch."

The Queen blinked several times, then looked at Ben. "Martin and Franklin?"

"Buried at the top of that hill." Ben pointed behind the house.

Behind the Queen, Flora set her hand on Marcel's head. She blinked, fury in her face as she turned to face her Queen.

Ignoring Flora, the Queen stepped toward Nate. "Martin was my mate; Franklin my son. I'll kill you!" The Queen leaped at Nate.

Just as Nate lined the Glock up for his shot, Flora jumped between them. "You murdered my mother."

Nate barely kept from pulling the trigger. He swallowed and pointed the gun at the ground, watching.

Lorena tried to brush past Flora. Flora caught her dress, pulled her around, and shoved her back. "I challenge!"

Everyone froze. Lorena slowly stood straight and turned to face Flora. "Kitten, this once, you may recant."

"I am not your kitten. I challenge. You have no right to be clowder Queen."

Nate heard Ben swallow. "Flora, don't . . . .."

"It is my right to challenge." Though it was obvious Flora spoke to Ben, she never took her gaze off Lorena.

136

Nate glanced at Koreth. *Challenge?*

Among were, a challenge for leadership is a battle to the death.

Nate frowned. *I can't allow . . ..*

You must. Koreth moved to stand between Nate and the two feline women.

He's right, Nate. Janelle slipped her hand into the crook of his left elbow. *You must allow this. Council law requires it.*

Nate sighed and shook his head. *So, what do we do, then?*

I will command. Koreth stood on his hind legs. *As Wolf of the Alpha, I command this battle be removed to the pasture beyond.* Koreth slapped his paws together. Nate saw nothing happen but felt a strong compulsion to obey.

As if they had no control over their own bodies, the werepanthers and werewolves followed Koreth's two-legged walk to the pasture. Koreth touched the gate. A glow extended from his paw and settled over the latch. The gate swung open. *Only the challengers may enter through. On pain of death, all others will remain on this side of the fence.*

The werecats lined the fence rail to witness the battle; the werewolves spaced themselves behind the cats. Ben and Marcel at his side, Nate closed the gate.

It begins. At Koreth's command, the two women snarled and leaped at each other, shifting to panthers in mid-air.

Chapter 26

Ben's hands cramped with his grip on the fence rail. Marcel crouched at his feet, muscles tense, ready to pounce, his tail straight behind him. Next to Ben, Nate stood shoulder-to-shoulder, offering what support he could. Ben appreciated the thought but was not able to even look his thanks to Nate. His sole attention was locked on his daughter as she and Lorena rolled in the grass fighting a deadly battle.

So intent was he on the fight, he forgot to breathe and after a moment felt light-headed. Having his only daughter in a death battle was bad enough. Having his only daughter in a death battle with the cat that killed her mother was worse.

Nate's hand gripped his shoulder and squeezed. "Breathe, Ben. You can't help her if you pass out."

Without removing his gaze from the battling cats, he nodded and forced himself to take deep, slow breaths. Flora's panther flipped the Queen to her belly and straddled her. Her mouth closed over the Queen's neck. At that moment, another panther screamed and bolted over the fence. Before Nate could do anything to stop him, Marcel shot under the lowest fence rail and caught the intruder in mid-leap. Both cats hit the ground rolling and fighting.

Flora's panther snapped her jaws, severing the Queen's spinal column, and shook her. With a final snarl, the Queen died. Standing over her dead adversary, the panther turned to inspect the pair fighting between her and the fence. *Enough!* Her thought blasted out to the pair, and they rolled away from each other. Marcel and Ben watched as she stalked over to the male who attempted to interfere with her fight. For a moment, she just looked at him, then her massive paw swiped his face, leaving deep, jagged marks dripping blood. *Shift now!*

The cat she clawed changed into his human form. Moments later, Flora shifted also. "By Clowder Law, I claim the title Clowder Queen. Bow."

The man pressed his hand to his bleeding face and stood in sullen defiance. Ben ground his teeth but knew his daughter must deal with the rebellion if her claim was to hold.

"Your mother gave me the opportunity to change my mind, Jeff. I give you the same chance. Bow."

He shook his head. "You are promised to me."

"I did not promise. As Queen, I choose my Tom."

Still, he refused, instead, spitting at her.

Flora's expression hardened. "As you choose." With a single nod, Flora reached up. Her forefinger shimmered into a claw. She clawed a deep mark on his face from his forehead to the bridge of his nose. "You are banished. If I or my clowder see you again, your life is forfeit. Be gone."

He glared at her, but turned and left, shoving through the gate Nate opened. Slamming his shoulder into Ben, he jerked a hunting knife from his belt and lunged toward the older man. Before he could plunge the knife into Ben's chest, Koreth caught him from behind. Teeth buried in the man's neck, Koreth shook him until he dropped the knife, then closed his jaws tight, not releasing until the man stopped moving. When he dropped the werecat in the dirt, no one moved for a moment.

Bury them with the others, Ben.

139

Startled, Ben nodded. "As you command, Alpha."

Flora pushed into Ben's arms. "Daddy!" She sounded like a lost child wailing in the dark. Ben didn't even try to stop the tears that came to his own eyes. Flora believed for so many years that he had killed her mother. She believed a lie. Guilt whipped through him. He hadn't tried to check on her, for fear Lorena would make good on her threat to kill his only child.

"I am so sorry, Baby." Ben cradled her in his arms, letting her cry against his chest. "It's okay, Flora. It'll be okay, now."

Chapter 27

Nate waited until father and daughter both stopped weeping, then cleared his throat. Even shorter than Janelle was, the young woman sniffed and looked up at him. Lips pursed, head tilted, Nate didn't know whether to call her Queen or Your Highness, so he just didn't. He cleared his throat again. "It's time to make some decisions."

The young Queen took a shaking breath, then stepped away from her father. Turning to face Nate full-on, shoulders back, she studied him. "What decisions, Alpha?"

"Your previous Queen was determined to have this ranch." When she opened her mouth, he held his palm toward her. "Before you speak, listen."

Flora glanced at her father and back at Nate. She pressed her lips together into a tight line and nodded.

"This ranch belongs to my pack. We will fight to protect it." Eyes narrowed, Nate watched her. "What are your plans?"

Flora took a long breath, and let it out just as slowly. She turned to face her clowder. As one, they bowed to her. Nate's eyebrow climbed into his hairline as she turned back and briefly bowed her head to him. "Our former Queen was greedy and, unknown to me, at least, a murderer. She has been punished. However, I know that your pack has suffered greatly at the hands of the clowder. You have my apologies. What restitution do you require?"

"Before we go further with this discussion, I want your personal guarantee that none of my pack will be attacked or harmed in any way. Do I have that?" When shame

141

stained her face with red, Nate almost felt sorry for her.

"You have my guarantee that none of my clowder will do anything to harm any member of your pack." She turned to the clowder. "So, say I."

"So, says the Queen," the werecats repeated after her, heads bowed. She nodded and turned back to Nate.

"And now, Alpha?"

"Now, we talk."

Chapter 28

Paisley set coffee cups and napkins before each person in the dining room. Lisa carried a pot of coffee into the room. Nate, Janelle, Jonathan, Ben, Flora, and Will, one of the toms appointed by Flora, were sitting around the large farm-style table. After Lisa served coffee, she set the coffee carafe on the table. Paisley brought a tray containing sugar and cream. Leaving the tray next to the carafe, Paisley followed Lisa from the dining room.

A pensive silence filled the room. After Flora's promise, Koreth commanded the wolf pack to become one with their humans, so this meeting was human, though the panthers and wolves watched the proceedings. Nate took a sip of his coffee, then set his cup down.

"Was greed the only reason your Queen made a move on the ranch?"

Flora glanced at Will. The two seemed to discuss her answer silently. Nate was starting to believe that she wouldn't answer when she turned back to him. "Lorena was greedy for things she shouldn't have. She cheated a powerful werebear in a business deal. He appealed to the Were Council. They decided in his favor, so our clowder lost its home to the werebear tribe."

Werebear? There are werebears, too? In his mind, Nate could hear the pack wolves laugh in short yipping barks. Koreth answered him. *There are many were. You will learn.*

Nate looked to his right. Janelle's lips rolled between her teeth, but her eyes were dancing. He shook his head and turned back to Flora. "So, all this was because your clowder didn't have a home?"

Flora bowed her head, her face again stained with embarrassment. She sighed and nodded. "It was."

Nate drummed his thumb on the table until he realized the eyes of every attendee were watching his hand. He stopped the drumming. "How many of the clowder were involved in the killing here?"

"I do not know for sure, Alpha. I think it was only Martin and Franklin. I will find out." Her gaze became unfocused as she turned her thoughts to her clowder. After several moments, she looked up at Nate. "Lorena, Martin, and their sons, Franklin and Jeffrey, were the only panthers involved in the murders of your pack."

Nate's eyebrow twitched when Koreth commented. *She speaks the truth.*

It was obvious to Nate that Flora was both ashamed and embarrassed by her former Queen's actions. He glanced at Janelle. *This was your home, your family. What do you think should be done?*

Anger and pain flashed across Janelle's face, but when she turned to look at the repentant Queen, compassion entered her eyes. Nate watched her study Flora, then she bowed her head. *Those responsible have been punished. I will not demand Council intercession.*

Council intercession? Nate looked inward to Koreth for an explanation.

The Council has the authority to condemn the clowder. Koreth's thought was grim. *If they are invoked, for a crime of this magnitude, they would apply maximum sentence. The clowder would die.*

Breath caught in Nate's chest. *All of them?*
All of them.

Nate leaned toward Janelle, cupped her face in his

144

hand and raised her chin so he could see her eyes. *This decision should be yours.*

Tears gathered in her eyes. She blinked repeatedly but kept her gaze locked to Nate's. "I have no wish to destroy the clowder. Enough children have died."

Flora and Ben both released a shuddering breath when Janelle spoke. Nate noticed but did not let it show. Instead, he kept his gaze on his mate. "What would you have me do?"

Janelle swallowed and blinked again. *Randal bought some property in East Texas, over close to Piney Woods, last year. We aren't using it for anything*

You want to give it to them?

No. For the pride of the clowder and the pride of the pack, offer to sell it to them. For the going price in the area. Don't try to make a profit, but don't cheapen the gesture, either.

Nate sucked air through his teeth. He nodded, released Janelle's face, and turned to Flora. "The pack has property in East Texas we would be willing to sell." He almost smiled at the startled look on Flora's face.

"You would offer this instead of calling Council?"

"We have decided not to invoke the Council." Nate gestured around the table at his pack members. "No one here wants to see more death. Those guilty have been punished. The clowder is innocent." He leaned forward and rested his elbows on the table, left hand clasped in his right hand. "I don't know what the land is worth, or even how many acres it is . . .." He arched an eyebrow at Janelle.

"Three hundred acres."

"Okay. Again, I don't know what this three hundred acre property is worth, what is on the land, or even if it has been improved upon, but we will sell it to the clowder for what it is appraised at." He glanced at Ben. "If you want to help them get settled there, you have leave to go."

Ben released a pent-up breath and nodded. "I am grateful, Alpha." He reached over to cover Flora's hand with his.

Flora bowed her head. "Your kindness and generosity are unexpected and much appreciated. However, when we lost our homes, our funds were also confiscated." Her voice caught, then she continued, "I'm not sure we can get a loan for the property."

"Well," Nate drew out the word, then grinned at Ben. "If you will stand as guarantor to the loan, Ben, I don't see any reason we couldn't carry the note ourselves."

Blinking rapidly, Flora's mouth dropped open. "You would do that?"

"Why not? I understand that we have the funds to do it. I trust your father, so if he will guarantee the loan, we will have a realtor get a value estimation and draw up the contract."

"On what terms?" Suspicion dripped through her question.

Ben cleared his throat. "Wait. Before this goes any further, I have something to say." When the room became silent, he swallowed and gave a small grin. "I've been working the same job for thirty-five years. I had no need for nice cars, fancy clothes, or other fineries, so I invested every dime I could." His grin turned sheepish. "I still have a few centuries to live, if I'm careful, you know."

Nate's eyebrow quirked. "And . . .."

"And if the price isn't more than a million or so, I think I can probably pay for the property outright, with

146

your permission, Alpha."

"My permission?"

"When you accepted me into the pack, my belongings became pack property."

Nate leaned back in his chair and stared at Ben. *Everything belongs to me?*

Janelle nodded, and Koreth agreed. Both thought, *Everything.*

"Okay. New pack rule. Anything anyone in the pack has worked for and earned himself belongs to him . . .." He glanced at Janelle. "Or her," he amended at her raised eyebrow, then grinned at her. "The pack will take a percentage, say . . . twenty percent of all earnings to go toward support of the pack." He glanced around the table at his pack councilors. "Acceptable?"

Janelle laughed. Jonathan snickered, and Ben grinned.

Janelle slipped her hand into the crook of his arm. "You are Alpha, Nate. Whatever you decide to do is pack law. If you want to let pack members keep eighty percent of their earnings, it happens."

"Just like that?"

Jonathan leaned forward and spoke for the first time since the conference started. "Just like that. In the pack, your word is law."

Nate shook his head and shrugged. "If you say so." When he looked back at Flora and Will, he almost laughed at the confusion on their faces. "Your father can explain everything after the meeting. Will you accept your father's funds to purchase the property in East Texas?"

Confusion still in her expression, Flora turned to look at her father. "Are you sure? You don't owe the clowder anything."

Ben patted her hand. "You are my daughter. How could

I not invest in your future?"

A single tear slipped out of Flora's left eye and slowly traced down her cheek. "You are a member of the wolf pack."

"I am, but I was your father, first."

Nate's thumb started drumming the table. Every eye again focused on his hand. He stilled his hand and sighed. "Ben, you should be with your daughter. You two have lost too much time, already." He pursed his lips, leaned back in his chair, and stared at the ceiling. Suddenly, he sat forward. "You are my special envoy, Ben. You are assigned to help her get the clowder situated in their new home. It should take you, oh, I don't know, at least ten or twenty years to get everything done. As our pack representative, you will, of course, keep me apprised of your progress. Say a monthly report. Satisfactory?"

Ben was momentarily speechless. He blinked several times and looked at Flora. When she nodded, he grinned at her, then looked at Nate. "I would be honored to be special envoy to the clowder."

"Good." Nate clapped his hands and rubbed them together. "It's been a long time since breakfast. Let's find something to eat."

"Nate." Ben swallowed, then pushed forward in a rush. "May I bury Lorena and Jeffrey on the hill with the other cats?"

Nate nodded. He felt his face burn with embarrassment. He couldn't believe he forgot the dead. "You may. The wolves will leave you to your service, but we will not attend."

Beyond Ben, Flora bowed her head. "Our thanks, Alpha." She stood. With a nod to Will, she turned and walked out of the dining room, Will on her heels.

Ben watched her leave, then looked at Nate. "My thanks, too."

Nate frowned and fixed his gaze on Ben. "Just one question. What do we do if anyone ever finds their graves?"

"That won't be a problem, Nate. When werepanthers die, after they are buried, their bones break down into the soil. In a few weeks, there will be no sign that there were ever bodies buried there." He shrugged. "If *were* left bones behind, we would have been discovered by humans many centuries ago."

With a sigh, Nate looked at Janelle. "It seems there is an awful lot I need to learn."

She nodded. "There is, but now you have time to learn."

Ben excused himself. At Nate's absent-minded nod, he slipped out the door to go help the clowder bury their dead.

Nate sucked air through his teeth and looked at Jonathan. "That leaves me short an advisor. Suggestions?"

"The boys are too young, and not yet tested." Jonathan seemed to hesitate. "Why not ask Janelle to be an advisor? She could take charge of the kids, while you determine how to proceed."

At Janelle's startled look, Nate raised his eyebrow. "You don't want to be an advisor?"

"The Alpha's mate is not usually asked to sit in the pack council." She picked up the napkin next to her untouched coffee and started shredding it into a small pile of paper strips on the table in front of her.

Nate watched. Her emotions roiled inside her, taking his breath at the pain he felt from her. He caught her hands in his, willing her to look at him. Her gaze lifted to meet his. Nate raised both her hands to his face and pressed a kiss to the back of each. "I won't require you to be an advisor if you don't want to."

"I pulled you into all this without even asking you if it's what you wanted." She swallowed hard.

Nate frowned at the tears pooling in her beautiful blue eyes. His thumbs stroked the backs of her hands. "I haven't complained." When she opened her mouth, he shook his head. "While I deeply regret the reason we came to be together, and I am so sorry for your losses, I cannot and will not ever regret meeting and mating you."

Jonathan cleared his throat. Nate glanced at him and nodded when the other man tilted his head toward the door. As Jonathan left the room, Nate pulled Janelle into his lap and pressed a gentle kiss to her forehead. He held her close until he felt her relax against him, then he leaned back to see her eyes. "Think about it, love. You do have a choice in this."

Janelle nodded and leaned her face on his shoulder. "I will be happy to take charge of the young ones, Nate."

Nate stroked her hair while listening to her muffled words. "But I need to tell you . . .."

Pups! In Nate's mind, Koreth howled, the sound joyful. *We are having pups!* In the back of his mind, Nate could hear the pack wolves joining in on Koreth's howls.

Stunned, Nate cupped Janelle's face in his hands and searched her expression. "You're pregnant? After just one night? And you can already tell?"

Janelle gave him a timid smile and nodded. "I wanted to tell you myself."

We are having pups!

150

Nate laughed. "I think Koreth is too excited to wait for you to tell me."

"And you, Nate? Are you excited?"

Nate looked at her and felt a slow smile take over his features. "I am," he whispered, then captured her lips in a long, possessive, yet tender, kiss.

The next book in the Texas Ranch Wolf Pack Series is *Wolf's Claim*.

Thank You!

Thank you for reading the first book in the Texas Wolves series. Learn more about books coming out soon: http://www.lynnnodima.com

Please Leave a Review

Reviews are the lifeblood of books in today's market. If you read this book, please take the time to leave an honest review where you purchased the book. Reviews are not book reports, they are just a few words to let others know how you liked or didn't like the book. Authors, especially indie authors, depend on their readers to let others know what they think of the book. Good or bad, reviews help authors on their publishing journey.

You can find Lynn's books and stories at:
www.lynnnodima.com

Lynn's Books

The Texas Ranch Wolf Pack Series
Wolf's Man
Wolf's Claim
Wolf's Mission
Wolf's Huntsman
Wolf's Trust
Wolf's Reign
Wolf's Queen
Wolf's Enemy
Wolf's Rage
Wolf's Quest
Wolf's Guard
Wolf's Duty

Texas Ranch Wolf Pack World
Wolf's Sorrow
Wolf's Son
Wolf's Mate
Wolf's Heart
Wolf's Dragon
Wolf's Princess

Texas Ranch Wolf Pack Box Sets
Wolf's Destiny: Books 1-6
Wolf's Destiny Volume 2: Books 7-12

More Fiction by Lynn Nodima

Tala Ridge Shifters
Tala Ridge Alpha
Tala Ridge Storm

Anthologies
Dreams in the Night

Short Stories
Alas, Atlantis!
All I Done
Design Defect
Heart Failure
A Relative Truth
Trinity's Sorrow
The Viper Pit

Visit www.lynnnodima.com to learn more!
Email Lynn at author@lynnnodima.com!

If you enjoy billionaire romances, check out Lynn's
Clean Romances: www.lynnscleanromances.com!

Made in the USA
Las Vegas, NV
08 April 2023

70362538R00094